"A Succulent Peace," is a must read! I could not put it down! I could definitely relate. If you have ever been in an abusive relationship, you must read this. This book gave me a reason to smile. It showed me that I deserve so much better....

Priscilla F.

The book made me very emotional. Some parts of the book brought back memories of my earlier life experiences. The more I read the more I could not wait to read the next chapter to see what was going to happen next.

JoAnn Williams

I thought the book was well written. I think the message is to have hope. Sometimes we have to take that first step in order for a change to take place. We have to ask for what we need in life. It is always important to have a good support system. I believe love will find you will find you when you least expect it. I recommend this book to anyone who may be struggling with issues in their lives that they may know that there is a rainbow after the rain....

Emma Freeman

A very relatable, feel good story with lots of spicy moments....

Raine

K. Dion is an insightful and gifted writer....

Angela M.

Excellent read! Enjoyed the book....

Ellen B.

It was AWESOME! The ending was perfect....

T. Daniel

I enjoyed the book. K. Dion is very talented....

M. Ricks

"A Succulent Peace," is what every person should have and need in their life. This book took me to places that I thought about going to and yet I got lost in the moment while reading the story because I thought I was there in that moment. To know that true love is out there means it can happen if you allow it to happen. Very detailed from the beginning to the end. Excellent story!!!!!

Danielle M.

"A Succulent Peace," is an excellent read!!! I recommend everyone read it! K. Dion is a great author.

Raeven H.

The book was Awesome! It is really good....

B. Sutton

It was very good. Writing is exactly what author K. Dion was meant to do....

S. Sutherland

"A Succulent Peace" is a powerful story about perseverance, hope, love, and family. This book takes you on a journey. It is a heartwarming must read for anyone who has suffered from abuse, low self-esteem, or a lack of hope.

A Succulent Peace

K. Dion

hollowvisionsllc@gmail.com

ISBN-13: 978-0-578-67056-0

DEDICATION

This book is dedicated to any woman who has been or is currently being abused in any way. Stay positive, be strong, and never give up. Just know that you do not have to remain in an abusive situation. Keep hope alive and believe in yourself. Keep your head up and find the courage to leave.

SPECIAL THANKS

A special thanks to five great women who had a positive effect in my life. They, directly and indirectly, molded me into the person I am today. These monumental women taught me to never give up or quit, to always hold my head up, to be proud of who and what I am, to never stop pursuing my dreams no matter what, to treat people with respect, and to have compassion for others. These wonderful women are Mary Holloway, Emma Trice, Virginia Holloway, Mary Upchurch, and Esther Carter. Thank You for taking care of me, believing in me, and showing me love.

Hidden Objects   Gospel Songs   Candy Canes   Orange Sherbert

Silently Strong   Peaceful

Religious   Survivor   Peppa

Selfless   Patient   Cornbread

Mary Holloway

Caring   Determined

Mobile Home

Mother   Church

Sacrifice   Big Heart   Basketball   Great Cook

California Love   Homebody   Walmart   Puzzles

Hardworking   Christmas Lights   Pineapples

Negro Spirituals

Funny

Deuteronomy

Peppermint Candy

Fly Swatter

Brown House

Flowers

Religious

Fiesty

Boweeba

Proud

Smart

Wigs

Emma Trice

Independent

Caring

Candy Lady

Loving

Granny

Church

Outhouse

9 Lives

Bible

Coloring Books

Dancer

Miracle

Apple Trees

Pace Board

Nigga in the Woods

Make Hace
Wrap Around Switch
1st Lady
Bible
Plum Trees
In Control
Relligious
Queen
Flamboyant
Caring
Virginia Holloway
Church
Expressive
Grandma
Boss Lady
Matriarch
Strong
Disciplinarian
Church Hats
Flowers
Comforter

Accepting of Everyone Generous

Independent Patient Wendy's Van Positive

Caring **Mary Upchurch** Survivor

Guardian Angel 2nd Mom Loving Spirit

Strong Big Heart Sacrifice Unselfish

Cadillac Girl Scout Cookies

Reasonable
Wonderful
Amazing Smile
Peace
Love
Kind
Positive

Esther Carter

Caring
Survivor

Shining Light
Angel
Honest

Amazing
Understanding
Loving Spirit
Mini Afro

Sweet

"I Love You Like a Fish Love Water"

CONTENTS

1	Emancipation	1
2	New Discoveries	10
3	Friendly Manipulation	23
4	Mysterious Situations	32
5	Handy Renovations	43
6	Strokes of Paint	53
7	Ocean's 2012	60
8	Marinating in the Sauce	72
9	Anatomy of a Motorcycle	82
10	Property of Mine	94
11	Mural of Time	105
12	Land of Dreams	113

www.hollowvisions.com

ACKNOWLEDGMENTS

The following people helped contribute to the production of this book. I would like to acknowledge them and give them credit for their contributions. Thank you for your help and support.

C. Stokes
Chapter 1-3 idea modifications and character development.

Raeven Hocutt
Chapter 8 ideas and development.

Emily Matthews
Poem "What is a Soulmate"

Kendrick Holloway
Poem "I Love and In Love"
Book Cover Design
Book Layout

George E. Woodbery
Failure Quote

Sajid Ali on Unsplash.com
Front Cover Photo

D. McCain
Editing Advisor

Defeat is not the worst of failures.
Not to have tried is the true failure.

George E. Woodberry

CHAPTER 1
Emancipation

It was a cold, and dreary February morning in *Scranton, Pennsylvania*. The temperature was a bone-chilling 15 degrees. I was on my way to my friend Sara's house to drop off my 10-year-old kids, Connor and Morgan. Sara volunteered to watch them because it was a teacher workday and I was on my way to divorce court. She did not have any kids of her own, so it was always a treat for her to spend time with them.

My kids are fraternal twins and the true loves of my life. Both of them were a little sad and nervous, due to all of the stress of the pending divorce and not knowing what the outcome will be. The kids love their Dad but they do not want to live with him. The possibility of me not being in their everyday life terrifies them even more.

After kissing the kid's goodbye, I headed to the courthouse to meet with my lawyer. Finally, there was going to be an end to the living hell I have lived through the past ten years.

I never thought I would be getting a divorce or that this day would ever come. I was so in love with Steve in the beginning and just never envisioned not having him in my life.

It seemed like decades ago when I first met him coming out of a *Michael's Arts and Crafts* store. Steve was walking by as I was dropping the handful of art supplies I was carrying.

He stopped and asked, "Do you need any help?"

As he spoke, I turned and was drawn to his eyes. Instantly a warm uncontrollable feeling came over my whole body. His hair was jet black and his eyes were sea blue which, rendered me speechless. I could not even utter one word. His eyes just seemed to grab me and put me in a hypnotic state.

When I finally gathered myself, he extended his hand and introduced himself as, "Steve Roberts."

I responded, "Nice to meet you. My name is Meadow Larson." At that time, he was a very helpful and courteous man. We ended up exchanging phone numbers and we dated for a year before getting married.

In the beginning of our marriage Steve was romantic and respectful. He was my rock and my comfort zone when I was feeling down. We were together all the time. I just knew I had found my *Superman.*

Things changed quickly after two years of marriage. Especially, when it was confirmed that I was pregnant. Steve began to stay out late and began to drink all the time. There were several occurrences after the kids were born that I would not see him for multiple days at a time and communication just completely stopped. He was always too busy with a big case that took all of his time. Eventually, he just stopped spending anytime with me or the kids.

A small part of me still loves him, despite the physical, mental, and verbal abuse I had to endure. I do not know why I still love him but I guess I inherited that trait from my Hippy parents. Do not get me wrong, I am happy and will be relieved when the divorce is final but at the same time I am scared to death.

Starting over and the uncertainty of the unknown just seems like it is going to be so hard. Doing it without a man being there just seems like a daunting task. Especially, since I am in my mid 40's now. I just do not know if I can live without a man in my life.

I say this because I have never had to pay one bill or deal with anything involving money. Steve took care of all of the bills himself. I do not know how to go about paying any bills or taking care of a household financially. Especially, after living with my parents until I got married. They took care of everything for me. I did not have to pay any bills while I lived with them either. I just wonder, "Where will I go? What will I do? I have not had a job in 12 years."

I parked the car and my mind began to wonder again as I began my long walk towards the steps of the courthouse. I began to question myself, "What did I do wrong? How did we end up this way?" I made my way through the doors of the courthouse and through the security checkpoints. My attorney, Thomas Peters, greeted me on the other side. Thomas is an old college friend of mine but I call him Tommy.

Tommy spoke briefly, about how we were going to approach the case. Tommy's ultimate plan was to expose Steve's temper and expose him as a hothead.

Tommy informed me, "Do or say whatever is necessary to hit a nerve to ensure we get a reaction from him."

We then proceeded into courtroom #3. I walked through the doors and there was my soon to be ex-husband, the infamous Steve Roberts. He was sitting there with his attorney and longtime college friend, Peter Swanson, whom he always referred to as Pete.

All of a sudden, a sick feeling came over me as I threw up a little in my mouth. Steve turned around and looked at me with eyes of disgust, as Tommy and I made our way to the table. There were several reasons for the hateful expression on Steve's face. The main one was probably because of the embarrassment or shame this may bring to his family.

Steve's father is a prominent and famous business person in the town of *Scranton*. He is so popular and well liked that if he chose to run for Mayor, he would win by a landslide.

Not long after we sat down, everyone had to rise for the Honorable Judge Thomas Hawthorne, who is one of only two judges in the whole county of *Lackawanna* who hears divorce cases. Judge Hawthorne has been hearing cases for more than 30 years. He is beloved throughout the county.

The divorce proceedings began with opening statements. Tommy outlined the physical, emotional, and mental abuse I endured during the 12-year marriage. He was followed by Pete's alleged accounts of how mentally unstable and unappreciative I was towards my husband and all that he had done for me. It became apparent that Pete was trying to paint a picture of me as an unfit mother.

I do not understand why he would do that. It was no way they could put that label on me. I had sleepless nights spent feeding, changing diapers, and just holding the kids while they were sick and crying. He had some nerve.

Steve really has never been in the kids' lives. He missed recitals, football games, school plays, and PTA meetings. Not to mention that this man has never once changed a diaper for either kid. I would be amazed if he even remembers their names.

Tommy called me to the stand and asked, "Can you tell the court about yourself and your background?"

I stated, "My name is Meadow Roberts and I am 44 years old. I am a stay at home Mom, not by choice, but because Steve did not want me to work. My husband felt that a woman's place was in the house not in the workplace."

Tommy asked, "Mrs. Roberts how did you feel about that?"

I answered, "I did not agree with it, but I went along with it anyway. I knew it would cause problems for us if I did not. I loved my husband and wanted our marriage to work, but marriage is not a one-way street. It is about compromise and sometimes sacrificing some of you for the good of the relationship or marriage."

"Before I met Steve, I was an Art Instructor at a local Community College for 12 years. I specialized mainly in painting. It is my first love and my passion. I have not painted anything in several years because Steve did not like or want me to paint."

Steve commented on several occasions that, "Painting is for crazy people."

Tommy continued by asking me, "Did Steve ever abuse you?"

I hesitated at first because I got emotional. I temporarily flashed back to the times of physical violence. Despite, fighting back tears, I proceeded to answer the question. I said, "Yes, I remember an occasion when Steve choked me until I was unconscious, just because I did not do what he wanted when he wanted it done. There were also several occasions when he verbally abused me in front of our friends and family."

Tommy asked me, "Did Steve ever abuse the kids?"

My response was, "Never physically or verbally but that was because he never spent any time with them."

Steve's attorney immediately objected, stating, "She did not answer the question."

Judge Hawthorne sustained the objection, and I was ordered to answer the question. My response was, "No, but he did neglect them."

Pete objected again, and again it was sustained. The Judge had my extra comments stricken from the record. Tommy was finished questioning me. Now it was Pete's turn to cross-examine. I did not know what to expect but I knew it could possibly be brutal. I felt they were going to attack my character, with made up lies and false accusations.

Pete approached the bench with a devilish smirk on his face. He thought he had me, but little did he know that I was ready.

Pete immediately asked, "Did you appreciate your husband?" Before I could respond, he said, "Because you did not have to work, pay one bill, and you lived comfortably in a nice house, during the 12 years of your marriage!"

I said, "Of course I did, but none of that means anything if there is no one to share it with you. In the beginning, I loved being married, but after the birth of the twins, it was like Steve was never there. If he was there, he acted as if he did not want to be. He always found some excuse to get away and leave."

The next question Pete asked was, "Have you ever had a nervous breakdown?"

My immediate response would have been, "Hell no!" but that would be what Steve and Pete would have wanted me to say to try to show I was unstable. I calmly said, "No, I have never had a nervous breakdown. It was not easy taking care of twins with no help, but I managed."

Pete asked, "How often did you and Steve have sex before the kids were born?"

I replied, "We would have sex every day several times a day."

Pete asked, "And after the kids were born?"

I said, "Only a few times that I can remember."

Pete asked, "Why was that?"

I was pissed with this question because I was always the one trying to initiate the sexual encounters and most of the time, I was rejected by him. I was not sure if he had found another woman or not, but I never had any proof that he was seeing anyone else either.

Even though Steve and I only had sex a few times after the kids were born, I was still faithful to my vows and never cheated on him during our marriage.

My answer to the question was, "Steve stopped being romantic and affectionate. He stopped caring about my feelings and needs. We only had sex when he wanted to, never when I was in the mood. The sex eventually just became meaningless. It lacked passion and love. It made me feel used and dirty, and I hated feeling that way. After a while, I just told him that I did not want to have sex with him anymore. He acted like he didn't care and just stopped trying which made my life a little easier."

"When I would have sexual impulses, I would do some form of exercise like Pilates. I never told Steve about me working out because he did not believe in me doing anything positive for myself. Looking back, I think he would have been happy with me just sitting in the house being a big fat slob. Apparently, he did not know I was not that type of woman."

I also stated that, "I would run a bubble bath, light candles, incense, and open a bottle of wine. I would put on relaxing romantic music, and pleasure myself, with my fingers, vibrators, or dildos for hours while the kids were sleeping."

Steve was incensed, and so embarrassed hearing this that he stood up with his face bloody red, and yelled, "You Fucking Cunt!"

Judge Hawthorne banged his gavel and demanded, "Order in the court!"

Finally, Pete asked me, "Why do you want a divorce?"

I concluded by saying, "I gave my all to my marriage, but I am tired of the physical, verbal, and mental abuse. I am tired of being lonely with someone who does not want to be with me or the kids. I'm tired of having someone else control, suppress, and dictate who I am. I am ready now to get back to being Meadow Larson. No matter what I may have to endure along the way. I just want to be me and to live free like my parents."

Pete concluded with, "I have no further questions of this witness." He then said, "I would like to call Steven Roberts to the stand."

Steve took the stand after being sworn in and stated, "My name is Steven Roberts and I am 46 years old. I am an attorney who works a lot of late hours to be able to provide nice things for my family."

Pete concluded by saying, "I have no further questions."

Tommy stood up, and did not waste any time asking Steve, "Why did you choose not to spend any time with your kids?"

Immediately, Steve's face started to turn red, and you could see that he was getting angry.

His response was, "How could I when I was working all of the time to provide a good life for them?"

Tommy asked, "How do you feel about a woman's place in a household?"

Steve said, "A woman's place is to stay at home, cook, clean, take care of the kids, and nothing more!"

Tommy concluded, by asking, "Did you ever abuse Meadow?"

Steve was so upset with the question that he stood up again and said, "Hell no, I have never hit that Lying Ass Bitch!" as he pointed at me the whole time.

Judge Hawthorne started pounding his gavel again and told Steve, "If you do not sit down, I am going to charge you with contempt of court!"

Tommy told Judge Hawthorne, "I have no further questions for the witness."

Tommy and Pete ended with conclusions reiterating their opening statements.

Judge Hawthorne said, "I will return to my chambers to ponder on who should get custody of the kids, child support, and how the property will be divided."

I headed to the bathroom, and I felt relieved. Even though Judge Hawthorne had not awarded me anything, it did not even matter. My happiness was about my kids, being free, and finally standing up to such an evil man.

When I returned to the table, Tommy was happy and excited about the way we were able to expose Steve's anger issues and how we were able to get under his skin.

About an hour later, Judge Hawthorne returned to render his decision. I received full custody of the kids, alimony, child support, and my car. Steve was allowed to keep the house and his car, but not before Judge Hawthorne lectured him on how to treat a woman.

He also assigned him community service at a battered woman's shelter. Ordering him to sit in and listen to the women's stories and how being abused affected their lives.

He also ordered Steve to volunteer at a Middle school and instructed him to spend time with kids the same age as Conner & Morgan. Judge Hawthorne's final orders was for him to take and complete anger management classes, and to attend *Alcoholics Anonymous* meetings on a weekly basis.

I was ecstatic and gave Tommy a big hug. I left the courthouse and headed straight to Sara's house to pick up Connor and Morgan. When I arrived, the kids were in the den watching their favorite show *Sponge Bob Square Pants*. They both ran towards me and hugged me around my waist. I assured them everything was going to be alright and we headed home.

CHAPTER 2

New Discoveries

One year ago, before our divorce was final; Steve moved out of the house, and was living at a local hotel. Judge Hawthorne ordered him to stay there for three more months. The same amount of time the judge gave the kids and myself to find a new place to live. After the three months Steve would be allowed to move back into the house. I was not sure where the kids and I would be living, but I knew for sure it was not going to be in, *Scranton, Pennsylvania.*

Once we arrived back home, I decided to call my parents. They live in *Key Largo, Florida.* I told them, "The divorce is now final, and we have three months to find a new place to live."

Immediately, without hesitation, Mom suggested, "Why don't you guys move to *Florida* with your Dad and I?"

I had contemplated moving with them once before but decided I needed to be on my own. It was important for me to not have to depend on anyone else again, as I had to do with Steve. I told Mom, "I will think about it and let you know in a few days, but I never did."

Several weeks go by, and I get a phone call. It is my Mom. I expected her to beg me to move with her and Dad, but she did not. Instead, she started talking about land, and a house they currently own. Apparently, it was left to her when her Mom, and my Grandma Lillie died of breast cancer eight years ago. Even though her name was Lillie we called her Ma Lillie. She lived in *Homestead, Florida.*

Mom continued to say, "The house has been vacant since her untimely death, and probably will need lots of work done to it. The kids and yourself are more than welcome to live there."

Dad got on the phone and told me, "We had the house and land on the market for several months, but we took it off the market after learning that you had to move out of the house in *Pennsylvania*. We feel that it would be a great area to raise the kids."

I was still hesitant about the whole thing but agreed to take a trip to see the property in person, before I made a final decision. I also thought it would be a nice change of scenery and a getaway for myself and the kids.

I hung up the phone, and part of me felt relieved, but at the same time, I was still scared. I called my friend Sara, who had been there for me the whole 12 years of my marriage. She was the only positive force that kept me going and probably the reason I was able to come out of the marriage with my sanity still intact.

Sara answered, and we began to talk about the kids. Eventually, I told her, "There is a possibility of the kids and myself moving to Florida." Before Sara could say anything, I started to cry and I told her, "I will miss you!"

Sara said, "I will always be just a phone call away, and I will visit you during the cold winter months of *Pennsylvania*."

I stopped crying long enough to tell her, "I Love You!" I then got off the phone, so I could go start dinner.

A couple of days went by and we began to pack for our trip to Florida. My parents paid for the plane tickets and wanted us to stay for two weeks. I made the decision to stay for only one week. I felt that would be more than enough time to see what we needed to see and get back to *Pennsylvania*. Plus, I did not want the kids to miss too many days of school.

Sara took us to the airport and sat with us until we boarded our flight. While we waited, I came to the realization that *Florida* could very well be our new home. The kids were so excited to be able to fly. They ran around the airport looking for planes taking off and landing. It was just the coolest, most amazing thing to them.

Before we boarded, Sara hugged me as if it was going to be the last time, we were going to see each other. Our first flight was about 41 minutes from *Scranton* to *Philadelphia*. Once we got to *Philadelphia* there was about an hour layover, before our connecting flight to *Miami, FL*. From *Philadelphia* to *Miami* was about four and a half hours.

Finally, the plane landed and we started to depart. I got so excited because I had not seen my parents in ten years. As soon as we exited the plane and entered the airport. There they stood all happy and cheery, just as I last remembered them. They both had on their tie-dye t-shirts. Dad had a long beard and ponytail. Mom's hair was long and flowing almost to her knees. Both of them were smiling and they seemed so free.

We all hugged, then I introduced them to the kids for the first time in person. Steve purposely kept me and the kids isolated from my parents. He even went as far as to tell my parents that they were not welcome in his home.

We made our way to baggage claim but it took a while for them to unload the luggage from the plane. It was ok because it gave Mom and Dad more time to get to know the kids as we waited. It felt great to see them together running around and laughing. It was like Mom and Dad were trying to make up for the ten years they missed.

After we got our bags we headed to Dad's car.

Dad mentioned to us, "It will be about a 47-minute drive to Ma Lillie's place in *Homestead, Florida*."

I have never been to Ma Lillie's new location so I was excited to see her house for the first time.

Mom said, "Ma Lillie use to live only a few miles away from the location we are going to now."

I can still remember spending summers with her and Grandpa Eddie. Those were the best of times. It is amazing after all of those years I still remember portions of how the land looked but have no clue of where to find it.

After Ma Lillie passed away Steve did not even allow me to go to her funeral because he did not want to pay for a plane ticket.

He also threatened me by saying, "If you go you will be going by yourself and you will never see the kids again."

This was part of his masterplan to keep me isolated from my family. I was so hurt and disappointed, but I still continued to do my part as a wife and Mother. My kids depended on me too much. I felt like I was the only one in the world they had to depend on.

We rode south from Miami for close to an hour, then Dad started to slow down. He signaled to make a right turn onto a gravel pathway that had a small wooden structure on the side of the road.

Mom said, "That structure was where Ma Lillie would be up bright and early every morning trying to sell her fruits and vegetables."

Finally, we were at Ma Lillie's house. We made our way up the long gravel pathway that curved slightly to the left. I could not help but notice the vast enormity of the land.

Dad commented, "The land is around 20 acres."

It was just amazing to see the long pathway lined on both sides with tall *West Indian Mahogany* trees.

I could not tell how big the house was but from what I could see it looked like it had a porch that wrapped around the entire house. It was white and you could tell that it needed some paint and some TLC on the outside. I could only imagine what it looked like on the inside.

The kids hopped out of the car and started running towards four large oak trees that lined the right side of the property. I did not understand why they were running or what they were running to or from, until I saw one of the oak trees with a tire swing hanging from it. I said to myself, "Lord, I have not seen one of those since grade school." Ma Lillie liked to entertain and always had something for everyone to enjoy.

Both kids jumped onto the tire swing. Dad hurried over to give them a big push. I began to make my way over and realized that I was crossing two horseshoe lanes. I remember as a young girl Ma Lillie and Grandpa Eddie playing. The whole family would play at family reunions, and they would even have tournaments. It was a big thing to them back in those days.

I watched the kids have fun and enjoy themselves as I took a seat on one of the picnic tables. They were between the tree with the tire swing and the last oak tree, which was closest to the pond. Ma Lillie apparently used the pond as a water source for her crops and animals.

We let the kids play for a while then Mom and Dad gave us a tour. There was a huge grill sitting between two large picnic tables. Several feet away in front of the pond were two swings that overlooked the pond.

Mom told me, "Ma Lillie would sit in those swings for hours just staring at the water. It did not matter if it was early in the morning or late in the afternoon. I believe your Ma Lillie would be reminiscing about your Grandpa Eddie during those times. She took his death really hard."

Walking halfway around the pond, we came upon a large building. It turned out to be a barn that contained Grandpa Eddie's tools and farm equipment. To the left of the barn was a large field.

Walking back towards the front of the house, we saw an assortment of apple, plum, and banana trees. We continued walking and made our way onto the porch. I saw that it really was in need of some repair. Several boards needed replacing, with many of them sticking up, warped, and squeaking as you walked on them.

I purposely let the kids and my parents go in ahead of me while I waited outside for about five minutes. I just did not want them to try and influence my decision about what we were about to see in any way. I wanted to experience it by myself then make a sound decision on what I thought was best for all of us.

Before I went in, I reflected on what I had already seen and I thought about if I could really envision the kids and myself living here. I opened the screened door and pushed the front door open, to the left was a large room that was used as a small store to sell Ma Lillie's cakes, pies, cobblers, and preserves. It still contained a few display cases, lots of shelving, and a counter that still had the original cash register that Ma Lillie used to collect the money. There were also several tables and chairs where customers would sit and eat their pie and cobbler and socialize.

Leaving the in-house store, my eyes were instantly drawn towards the stairs and a long hallway to the right that led to the kitchen. To the left of the stairs was a large open family room.

I headed towards the kitchen. I am not a cook but I do remember Ma Lillie being a great one. We would have a breakfast, lunch, and dinner buffet every day. Her pies and cobblers were the best. I was so anxious to see what her new kitchen looked like. It was large with lots of cabinets and was open to the dining room and family room with a bar top and island in the center of it. All of the appliances were new and updated.

I did not notice the screened porch while we were outside but the dining room had a door that led directly to it. This was where the kids were running around and playing with the switch to the ceiling fan, constantly turning it on and off.

I started to climb the stairs and when I got to the top, I saw two doors leading to two nice size bedrooms that shared a bathroom between them. When I saw them, I instantly thought that they were perfect for Conner and Morgan. I noticed in both bedrooms a small short door in the sidewalls. I did not know what the doors were for but just figured they led to some sort of storage space.

I opened the door in what was to be Conner's future room and it was a storage area with lots of storage space. I stuck my head in further and saw what I thought was a box, but it was too far back for me to reach. I called Conner over who was playing with Dad in the loft area and told him, "Crawl through the door and get the box." He crawled in and pulled out what I thought was a box but turned out to be a chest that had a lock on it.

I called for Mom to see if she knew what was in the chest. She looked just as surprised and intrigued as everyone else was. Mom did not know anything about it, nor did she have a key for it. Dad picked it up and took it to the car.

He said, "We will open it when we get back to the house."

After checking out the kid's bedrooms, I made my way over to the large open loft area. This is where I saw the door to the Master bedroom suite. The suite was very large with a trey ceiling in the middle of it. Walking through the suite, I came to the master bath. I entered the master bath and I was in awe of what I saw. This is my favorite part of any house but what I saw was unexpected. A toilet room with a door, his and her sinks with a desk area between them. There was a large jacuzzi corner tub with a flat screen tv on the wall. It also contained a large glass walk-in shower right beside it with a shower seat and four shower heads.

Mom said, "We had the kitchen and bathrooms remodeled hoping that would help the house sell faster."

At this point, I had seen all that I needed to see concerning the house. I had already made up my mind, but I was not going to reveal it to my parents or the kids until we visited some schools in the area. One other big thing for me was extracurricular activities for the kids outside of school. Conner played *Pop Warner Football*, and Morgan was a *Pop Warner Cheerleader*. It was important for me to find out if there were any local teams in the area.

We all headed to Dad's car, a 1996 *Buick Roadmaster Station Wagon*, as he locked up the house.

Mom told us, "It is about a 41-minute drive to *Key Largo* from *Homestead*."

Conner and Morgan fell asleep while Mom and Dad inquired about my thoughts of the house. I told them, "It all looked promising, but I had not decided yet." When we reached my parents' house, we woke the kids and we went inside. Mom showed us around while Dad brought in the bags.

It was a lovely five-bedroom house overlooking the ocean. Each of us had a room to ourselves.

Mom said, "I decorated each room specifically for each of you."

Mom decorating was not a surprise to me because she was an Interior Decorator before she retired. My room had a, "Meadow," theme with everything you could imagine that could be in a Meadow in this room. I saw different types of flowers painted all over the wall especially, lilies' because they were Ma Lillie's favorite flower. You could also see a few trees, birds, a windmill, and plenty of water. I went to check out the kid's rooms to see what my Mom's imagination had come up with for them.

Conner's theme for his room was, "Football." His bed was custom made with two field goal crossbars at each end. Hash marks and yard line designations were painted on the sides of the bed with several football jerseys hanging on the wall. On one of the dressers was a *Miami Dolphin* football jersey, shoulder pads, and a helmet autographed by the great *Dan Marino*. Conner picked up the helmet and looked at it in amazement. He placed it on his head and started to run around the room.

I left his room and headed to Morgan's room. The theme for her room was, "Cheerleading." There were cheerleading uniforms of every football team in Florida, both of college and professional teams hanging on the wall. There were also pom poms and silhouettes of cheerleaders in different cheer poses on her wall. On her bed was a cheerleading uniform of the *Miami Dolphins*. Morgan put it on and began to do some new cheers she had just recently learned. I told Morgan and Conner, "Make sure you unpack your things." Then I headed back to my room.

While we unpacked, Mom was cooking us some hotdogs and fries. It took the kids a while to come down because they were enjoying their rooms and all of the many surprises contained in them. We finally got them to come down and they ran to give Mom and Dad a hug, thanking them repeatedly for everything. We ate and the kids ran back upstairs to play.

I stayed downstairs to talk and catch up with my parents. It had been a long day, but it felt good to be able to sit and chat with them after all of these years.

A few hours later I began to get sleepy, so I gave my parents a kiss. I headed upstairs to make sure the kids took a shower and were ready for bed. I then headed to my room to take a shower myself and turned in for the night.

The next several days were spent traveling back and forth to *Homestead* and visiting different schools in the area. We did end up finding two potential schools and narrowed it down to just one. Both schools had high test scores, but the one we liked best offered more advanced college prep classes.

The kids enjoyed themselves the whole week. It really had been a long time since I had seen their faces so lit up with smiles. It made me feel good and helped to make my decision easier. Two days before we were scheduled to leave, I sat my parents down and told them, "I have made my decision."

They were anxious and excited. I started discussing the house first and told them, "I love it and I think it has a lot of potential, but needs some work done to it like repainting the inside and outside and redoing the porches."

I went on to say, "I am overwhelmed by the amount of land and everything on it. I do think it will provide an excellent stable environment for Conner and Morgan to grow up. I also feel that this is a place that they will thrive." I concluded by saying, "I have decided that we will be moving to *Florida!*" Mom, Dad, and the kids began to jump up and down and high five each other.

After everyone had settled down, Dad told us, "Tomorrow, I will give you a full tour of the town of *Homestead*."

The next day, my parents and the kids were up early and already dressed and ready to go. I went to the kitchen to get some breakfast. I quickly ate then went upstairs to shower and got ready. Dad drove us around for several hours showing us everything from the post office, the mall, the local ice cream parlor, and a flower shop.

Before we headed back to *Key Largo*, Mom wanted to pick up some things for dinner that night. We found one of the local grocery stores and went inside. The kids hopped in the cart with Mom and Dad and they took off.

I walked around by myself to see what the store had to offer. I went down a few aisles, and it was the same type setup as stores in *Scranton* until I walked down aisle #3. It contained spices and baking products.

In the distance, there was a man! A real man! He just had on a referee shirt, black *Nike* pants, and a whistle around his neck. I am very attracted to men in referee uniforms. I do not know why, but it is something about the sense of power and authority that does it for me.

The shirt was tight fitting and showing off every inch of his massive chest. His arms were bulging out of his sleeves and they were solid as a rock. They were not too big but big enough that you could see a portion of a vein forming down the middle of his bicep, as he pushed his basket towards me.

I don't know why but a warming sensation instantly came over my body. I immediately said, "Lord Jesus, sometimes you just have to pray!" as I was about to start rubbing my nipples. I had to snap back to reality and remember where I was quickly before anyone saw me.

He had short dark black hair with it spiked on the top.

He smiled at me with dimples as he walked by and said, "Hello."

I began to get moist instantly. I said, "Hello," then immediately turned to sneak a peek at his ass. With a chest and arms like that, he had to have a nice tight firm ass.

I was not disappointed as I started having visions of him on top of me, and me cuffing handfuls of his ass cheeks, as he was grinding and fucking me slowly. I know it has been years since I had any sexual encounter with a man, but this one man really turned me on. I have seen hundreds of attractive men during those years, but none of them made my body quiver the way that this one did.

I began to question, "Why am I feeling this way?" and, "Why him?" My first thought was to follow him because I wanted to see more. I wanted to talk to him, but I was nervous and did not want to embarrass myself. I debated for a few seconds on whether I should go around the corner to the next aisle or not.

I finally got up the nerve to talk to him. I turned the corner and saw he was in the frozen food section looking at ice cream. I walked up to him and asked, "What is your favorite flavor?" I was shocked that I was able to open my mouth, but this man had something special about him and I wanted to find out exactly what it was.

He responded by saying, "*Butter Almond*," and commented, "I like my ice cream slightly melted. Almost to the point where I can sip it out of the bowl then lick up all the nuts left over."

My legs became weak, I got lightheaded, and I almost fainted into his arms.

I laughed it off and introduced myself, "Hello, I am Meadow," as I extended my hand. He shook my hand and said, "My name is Dylan, and it is a pleasure to meet you."

I asked him, "What kind of sports do you referee?

He told me, "I do all sports, except football. I just finished refereeing a soccer game before I came here."

I said, "That is too bad because my son Conner loves to play football."

Dylan responded by saying, "That is great, because I am a *Pop Warner Football* coach for a 10-11-year-old boys team called the *Florida City Razorbacks* and our season starts in a few weeks."

He was talking but, I was not listening at all. My mind started fantasizing again, and this time he was naked in the shower with his body dripping wet.

Apparently, Dylan asked me several questions during my brief moment of day dreaming because when I snapped back to reality, he was asking me, "Are you ok?"

I told him, "I'm fine."

He then asked, "How old is Conner?"

I told him, "He is ten and he played tight end."

Dylan said, "Wow, I have a 10-year-old daughter myself." He reached into his pocket and pulled out a small piece of paper. He wrote down a phone number and stated, "This is my cell number give me a call tomorrow and I will let you know our scheduled practice times. How about you bring Conner to our practice this weekend? He could meet the team and even suit up if he would like to."

I quickly filled him in, "I do not live here, but we are in the process of moving here from *Pennsylvania*. We are going to be heading back there in the morning. I will keep your number and give you a call when we finish moving all of our stuff and get settled in."

Dylan welcomed me to *Florida* and told me, "Have a safe trip. I have to run so I can pick up my daughter Casey from cheerleading practice."

I shook my head and said, "This is too good to be true." Dylan looked at me with intrigue. I explained, "I have a 10-year-old daughter also and she is also a cheerleader."

Dylan said, "Amazing, well ok just give me a call so we can talk more."

I smiled and said, "I will." In my mind, I said, "I certainly will whether it concerned football or not."

Dylan headed toward the checkout area, and I said, "Lord & Jesus!" as I watched him walk across the floor with a confident swagger. I just love a confident man.

I went looking for my parents and the kids. It turned out that they were already in line to be checked out. We put the bags in the car and on the drive back to *Key Largo* I told both Conner and Morgan, "I met a guy named Dylan in the store and he is a *Pop Warner* football coach. He has a daughter the same age as both of you, and she is into cheerleading too."

The kids were excited and at the same time said, "We do not want to go back to *Pennsylvania!*"

I cannot say that I was shocked because of all of the fun they were having with my parents.

They repeatedly asked, "Do we have to go back? Can we stay here?"

I told them, "You will have to ask your Grandma and Grandpa."

Both of my parents said, "Of course, you can, we were going to suggest it to your Mom."

I said, "Ok, well it is settled! This will also allow me more time to tie up some loose ends and prepare for the move back here."

The next morning, we headed to the airport in *Miami*. After they dropped me off, I just stood there delighted as I watched my parents and the kids drive away. I reflected back on the trip and how everything went so well. I boarded the plane and was on my way back to *Pennsylvania*.

CHAPTER 3
Friendly Manipulation

On the plane, I could not get Dylan out of my mind, but I knew I had to focus on other things. The two most important things were getting everything packed and moving out of *Pennsylvania*. The kids and I had a great time in *Florida*, and I wanted to get back there as soon as possible.

When the plane landed in *Scranton*, I called Sara from my cell phone to let her know I had arrived. We had made prior arrangements for her to pick up the kids and myself from the airport.

Sara said, "Ok, I will meet you guys at baggage claim."

I told her, "It will be just me."

She said, "What you mean just you?"

I said, "Oh yea, I forgot to inform you that the kids loved *Florida* so much that they wanted to stay in *Florida* with my parents. I came back to make all of the necessary arrangements for us to move to *Florida*."

Sara was shocked and asked, "Why didn't you tell me that you had decided to move?"

Immediately, I said, "Sorry, I made the decision to move before I left *Florida*."

Sara said, "Congratulations," but it seemed as if she forced herself to say it.

I was puzzled why she was acting this way. I told her, "Bye," and headed to baggage claim as I hung up.

While waiting for my bag, I smiled to myself, as I could only imagine what my parents and the kids were doing. It was no telling with them, but whatever it was I am sure they were all having fun.

A few minutes went by, and I finally saw my bag, but when I reached for it, someone else grabbed it. I was about to get mad until I realized that it was Sara. We both laughed as I told her, "You were about to get pepper sprayed because I knew that bag belonged to me."

Sara gave me a hug and said, "I missed not having you around last week."

On the way home, I filled her in on everything that happened in *Florida*, especially the part about meeting Dylan.

Sara smiled at me and said, "That's great that you met someone," but again she just did not seem genuine to me.

For some reason, she was acting weird, and she just was not her usual happy-go lucky self. I started thinking to myself about what was going on and just blew it off. I figured she must have been tired or was just having a bad day.

Arriving at my house never felt as good as it did that day. Throughout ten of the twelve years of living there it felt like I was walking into a dungeon, every time I walked through the doors. The house just seemed to drain the life out of me in those past years. It felt good to walk through the same doors and not feel that way anymore. Knowing that I only had a short period-of time to be there made me feel even better.

Sara helped me bring in my bag, and I told her, "Thanks," as she headed back to her car. Apparently, she was on her lunch break and needed to get back to work. I closed the door and sat down on the couch for a few minutes just to relax. Instead of relaxing, my mind was filled with memories of the verbal abuse and the long lonely nights I had in this place. I regrouped and decided at that moment this was going to be the last time I would let those ten terrible years affect my life ever again.

I got up off the couch and felt so cleansed and relieved. I headed to the kitchen because I was getting a little hungry and made myself some chicken parmesan with a small salad. After eating, I headed upstairs to unpack my bag, called the kids, and turned in for the night.

The next day I woke up early. The first place I went was to Conner and Morgan's school to have them transferred to the school we chose for them in *Florida*. I left the school and went to the post office to fill out a change of address form, which was so liberating. Finally, I was going to be able to get out of the Town of *Scranton*.

My next move was to find a moving company capable of packing all of our things and getting all of our stuff to *Florida* with no problems. I researched several movers but decided to go with one that guaranteed that they would pack everything in two days and would get it to *Florida* safe. It was Saturday, so I decided to have them come Tuesday and Wednesday of next week.

My plan was to start driving back to *Florida* Thursday afternoon and arrive midday on Saturday. I scheduled the movers to arrive in *Florida* with our things Saturday afternoon. Having them arrive Saturday afternoon would give me a few hours to decide where I wanted everything. I also would be able to get the house cleaned up before they arrived.

A few days go by, and I had not heard from Sara since the day she dropped me off at my house. I was starting to worry that something was wrong, but I was going to give her some time and let her call me. Tuesday came and the packers and movers were at my door early and were ready to get started. By Wednesday afternoon they were finished and had everything packed neatly in the truck.

They left and I headed upstairs to take a shower until I heard the phone ring. I looked at the caller id and it said Sara McClain. I was hesitant to answer it at first, but then I thought about all of the times she listened and helped me with my problems when I called her in the past. I picked up the phone and said, "Hello." I did not know what I was about to hear from her.

Sara said, "Hello," then started apologizing. "I am so sorry for not coming by or calling since I dropped you off a few days ago. I needed some time to deal with losing my best friend to the state of Florida."

I told her, "It's ok. It is not easy for me either. I will always be just a phone call away. The same words you told me a few weeks ago."

Sara started to cry and insisted, "Please let me cook a nice dinner for you tomorrow before you leave."

I said, "I will agree only if you let me help you prepare the food."

She agreed and said, "I will see you tomorrow at my house around 6:30 pm."

I asked, "What do I need to bring?"

She said, "I just need you to bring yourself, and I will get everything else."

I said, "Ok."

We said, "Goodbye," and I hung up.

I took my shower and then called to check on the kids. Conner and Morgan sounded happy and excited. They started to tell me all of the things Mom and Dad had them doing and all of the places they had seen and visited. I told them, "I am so happy for you and I will be leaving tomorrow night to head back your way." We exchanged, I Love You's, and then I hung up. I cut off the lights and went to sleep.

I woke up late the next morning. Overseeing and directing what box was going to go in what room had really worn me out. My back was a little sore as I got up from the sleeping bag and went to use the bathroom. After taking a long hot shower, I went to a local family owned café. This café just happens to overlook the town. I would go there as often as I could because they had the best Danishes in town. I was really going to miss this place when I move.

I ordered a coffee and a *Praline Peach Danish*. I sat overlooking the town and thinking to myself that this view would make a beautiful mural painting that I could put up on the wall of my new home. I started eating my Danish and began to read the local newspaper that was sitting on the table. I flipped to the obituaries and began to browse through the names when I came across a name I recognized. Mrs. Mabel Andrews my high school art teacher. She was the one who always told me that I was talented and encouraged me to stick with art. I thought to myself for a minute and then said a short prayer for her because she was truly a great woman and mentor to me.

I took out my digital camera and took several pictures of the view. I finished my coffee and headed to *Wal-Mart* to gather some cleaning supplies. When I got back home, I unpacked the supplies and started to clean the kitchen and the bathrooms. After I finished, I was a little tired, and now every part of my body was sore. I cleaned up and got dressed to go to Sara's house.

It was about 6:00 pm now and Sara lived twenty minutes away. I needed to be leaving. I did not know what to expect from this dinner, but I was sure we were going to have fun. I arrived at her house and as I walked towards the door, I could smell the aroma of food. I was not sure if it was coming from Sara's house or from one of her neighbors.

I rang the doorbell and there was a brief pause then the door opened. Sara was standing there smiling and welcomed me to come in. I walked in and I could smell a floral fragrance but did not know what it was. I commented that, "Your house smells wonderful,"

Sara replied, "It is *Chamomile* scented incense and *Jasmine* scented candles."

I told Sara, "I am ready to help cook," without saying a word Sara grabbed me by my hand and guided me towards the dining room area. I looked at the table and it had already been set with two fancy plates, fancy silverware, a bottle of *Chardonnay* wine on ice, a lovely arrangement of yellow roses in a round vase, and four candles already lit.

She led me to my seat and pulled out the chair as I sat down. I told her, "You did not have to go through all of this for me." Sara walked over to the stove and brought back a plate of appetizers she had prepared. It just so happened to be my favorite appetizer, *Tomato Basil Bruschetta*.

After dimming the lights, the candles provided a soft glow that reflected off the wine glasses adding a romantic ambiance to the room.

Sara smiled as she sat down and said, "You are my friend, and I wanted to do something unique and memorable for you so let us celebrate."

I said, "Ok," as Sara poured us some wine and we toasted to me moving to Florida. We ate the appetizers, and I started telling Sara about the last couple of days of lifting, moving, cleaning, and how sore I was from it.

Sara said, "I am sorry I was not there to help you. How about you let me give you a massage later to help relieve some of your soreness."

I have never had a massage before, so I said, "Ok." Sara manages a massage parlor and is a certified masseuse. What did I have to lose? She gathered what was left of the appetizers and put them on the stove. On her return from the stove she had the main dish, which consisted of *Crispy Trout with Cilantro and Macadamia nut sauce*. There was also a side of *Roasted Rosemary Garlic Potatoes* and a *Tomato and Blue Cheese salad*.

I was shocked because I love seafood. I also remembered that I told Sara about the exact recipe several years ago. I just never tried it myself. It was incredible that she remembered it. We poured more wine and began to eat.

During the main dish, Sara started complimenting me on what I was wearing and how good I looked.

She told me, "I am so proud of you for the decision you made and you have my support 100%." Sara continued to say, "If there is anything you need just let me know."

All of those words were good to hear, and they made me feel good inside. A few days ago, I did not think that she felt this way.

When we finished eating, I headed to the living room. On the coffee table there was a large bowl filled with an assortment of different fruits and two smaller bowls filled with chocolate, along with another bottle of *Pinot Grigio* chilling on ice.

I grabbed a strawberry as I sat down then Sara sat down beside me. She grabbed a slice of pineapple, dipped it into one of the bowls of chocolate, and held it up to my lips, as she waited for me to open wide. I did and she placed it into my mouth in a very seductive way.

We both giggled and laughed at each other because we were always acting up and doing silly things like that. We ended up watching several comedy movies, drinking the whole bottle of wine, and laughing at everything. It was starting to get late, and I knew it was too late to head to *Florida*. I told Sara, "I am going to leave and head back to my house."

Sara said, "No, you forgot about the massage I promised you."

I said, "Yea, you are right. Plus, I am starting to feel a buzz from all of the wine. Maybe I will sober up by the time you finish the massage."

I thought she was going to do it on the couch, but Sara insisted we go upstairs.

She said, "I have a special massage room, but first give me a moment to set up," and headed upstairs.

She returned a few minutes later and escorted me upstairs. I was kind of hesitant at first, but said, "Ok," and headed up the stairs.

I was about to walk into the massage room but noticed the lights were off, soft music was playing, and there were candles lit up everywhere.

I turned and looked at Sara with intrigue, and she said, "All of this is important to set the mood for relaxation and full enjoyment of the massage."

I said, "Well you are the expert," and proceeded to go in the room. Sara was behind me carrying what was left of the bottle of *Chardonnay*, the bowl of fruit, and one of the bowls of melted chocolate.

She told me, "Go to the bathroom, where there is a robe you can change into,"

The robe actually had my name embroidered on it.

Sara told me, "You can strip down to your panties, or you can take them off."

I decided to leave my panties on and wrapped up in my new pink robe. I came out of the bathroom and she told me, "Lie down on the massage table."

The table was custom built specifically for the room.

I took off the robe and laid face down on the table because Sara said, "I am going to work your back first."

She started by placing heated towels over the lower half of my body to help keep me warm. I watched as she pulled out all different types of oils and put them on top of a table nearby.

Sara grabbed one of the bottles of oil and poured some in her hand and began to rub my back. The oil had a sort of vanilla smell to it. She began to rub it into my skin. After several minutes of rubbing I could feel the pain in my back slowly disappear. The more she rubbed the better it felt and the more relaxed I became.

I could not believe that she could maneuver her hands in that kind of way. I felt myself beginning to doze off. I shook my head and snapped out of it. Sara continued to rub my legs, arms, and my neck then asked me to turn over on my back and continued to rub my feet and legs.

Eventually, Sara made her way up my stomach and to my breasts. I was ok with that because she had touched my breasts before so I thought nothing of it. I closed my eyes and a few minutes later I felt something wet and warm on one of my nipples.

I was shocked, but before I could say anything or open my eyes, I felt a hand in my panties rubbing my clit, and It felt so good. Instead of getting mad I began to moan and thrust my hips in a forward and upward motion. I even started to rub my other nipple slow and gently with my fingertips. Sara continued sucking on the other one. I was overwhelmed and could not believe how good it felt as I began to cum all over Sara's fingers.

I woke up the next morning in Sara's bed. Both of us were totally naked and cuddled in a spooning position. I do not totally remember what happened that night nor was I going to ask, but all I knew was that I needed to find my clothes and get the hell out of here.

I managed to find my clothes and snuck out without waking Sara. I cried all the way to my house and repeatedly asked myself, "How could she do that to me? How could I be so naïve? and Why did I let this happen? I am not that way, I like men." I felt manipulated and ashamed.

When I got home, I immediately blocked Sara's phone number and took a bath, scrubbing every part of my body several times in hopes of cleansing away the shame I felt.

CHAPTER 4
Mysterious Situations

After thoroughly cleansing my body, I packed the last few things in my car and headed to the law office. One condition of the divorce being final was that I was supposed to turn over the keys to the house to Tommy. Tommy would then turn them over to Steve's attorney. I gave the keys to Tommy and thanked him for all that he did for me.

He told me, "I am happy for you and I wish you good luck." I turned to walk away, and Tommy said, "If you need anything do not hesitate to give me a call."

I told him, "I will," and proceeded to my car. I drove away and headed to the gas station. While my car was filling up, I went inside to pick up a few snacks, as I prepared for this twenty plus hour journey. I got on *I-95 South* and called my parents. I told them, "I am leaving later than expected, but I am on the way."

My parents said, "Ok."

I talked to the kids for a brief moment then I got off the phone. Several hours later I made it to *Florence, SC.* I decided to spend the night in *Florence* because it was halfway between *Scranton* and *Homestead.* I checked into my hotel then went to bring in my bags.

In the lobby I noticed a sign for a fitness center, so I decided that I was going to go work out. Working out in the past was my safe haven and getaway from what life was throwing my way. I especially needed it after the situation with Sara the night before. It replayed in my head over and over the whole 10 hours. I worked out for about an hour then headed back to my room to shower.

After getting dressed I was a little hungry. I drove down the road and got me some food. When I got back, I was exhausted, so I ate and went to bed. Waking up a couple of hours later I had a puddle of drool on my pillow, and the lights and TV were still on.

I left early that next morning and drove until I reached *Florida*, and the infamously long *Florida Turnpike*. I was sleepy again and did what I had to do to stay awake. I sang along with songs on the radio, sipped on coffee, and chewed on sunflower seeds. I had been on the *Florida Turnpike* for several hours when my gas light came on. I saw a gas station exit sign ahead, but before I could get off on the exit my phone began to ring and distracted me.

The call turned out to be from the kids. I was so excited to hear their voices that I decided I would bypass this exit and get off on the next exit with a gas station sign instead.

Connor and Morgan both expressed how much they loved and missed me. Those words were like music to my ears and was the fuel of motivation I needed to give me that extra boost to get me back to *Homestead*.

After I hung up the phone my gas light started to flash. I began to really get nervous and panic as I wondered how far away the next gas station really was. I rode another mile and finally saw a sign that indicated a gas and service station eight miles away. My heart started beating fast as I began to panic even more. I prayed and reflected back on how I should have gotten off on that exit when the kids called earlier.

After about four miles my gas light stopped flashing and went off. I began to pray even more and three miles later my car began to sputter then just shut down as I tried to get it off the road. After coming to a complete stop on the shoulder of the road, I cried for several minutes. My family was four to five hours away, and I had no one to call. I just felt so helpless.

Once I composed myself, I grabbed my bag and cell phone, locked the car, and began walking the last mile to the gas station. I was both nervous and scared. Some of the people driving by whistled and others screamed XXX rated obscenities.

There was one man in a truck who pulled off the road and offered me money to get in. I kept walking and had my hand on my pepper spray the whole time. Finally, he came to the realization that I was not going to get in and he drove away.

The temperature was about 95 degrees, but it felt as if it was 110 degrees. My shirt and shorts were both soaking wet. I took off my shirt, which left me with just a sports bra on. I took the shirt and threw it over my head to try to help shade my body from the baking sun.

When I finally made it to the service station, I headed straight to the Icee machine and made me a Cherry Icee. Before taking a sip, I rubbed the cup across my forehead and the back of my neck.

After cooling off, I took a few sips while walking down each aisle searching for a gas container. I finally found one and headed to the register. There were two men behind the counter. The first man was short with bifocals and stringy hair, he rang me up.

The second one just watched at first then asked me, "Mam, I did not see you pull up in a car, and I see you with a gas can, is everything ok?"

He looked like he was a mechanic by the uniform he had on but I was not sure. He had on a *Miami Marlins* baseball cap, with long dirty blonde hair sticking out the sides of it and was wearing coveralls. I did not want to answer, but at least he was offering services to help me instead of offering me money for sex.

I began to tell him, "I am on my way to *Homestead, FL* but my car ran out of gas about a mile away, and I had to walk here."

The man said, "Well mam, your luck is about to change. By the way, my name is Junior, but most people call me J.R. and it is wonderful to meet you."

I told him, "My name is Meadow Roberts."

J.R. said, "Well Mrs. Roberts I am going to give you a ride back to your car. First, we need to get you some gas."

I said, "Yes, you are right. Let me pay for it."

J.R. stated, "That's not necessary. There will be no charge."

He filled the gas can up, and we hopped in his wrecker truck, and headed to my car.

When we got to my car, J.R. put the gas in and I thanked him several times while offering him money but he still refused to take it.

Finally, he said, "Ok, if you come back to the station, fill up with gas, and pay for that, I will check all of your fluids and even change your oil, to ensure you a safe trip to Homestead."

I agreed, and we headed back to the station. While I waited for J.R. to finish with my car, I called my parents and informed them, "The movers will probably get there before I do. Please make sure that you are there when they arrive so you can unlock the door for them." I purposely did not tell my parents about what happened to me because I did not want them to worry.

I got back on the *Florida Turnpike* and after a total of twenty-three plus hours, I finally arrived in *Homestead*. I pulled into the long driveway and could see several of the moving company workers lifting and unloading our things. There was no sign of the kids or my parents. I parked on the side of the driveway and began to gather my bags from the car.

Shortly afterwards I heard some voices saying, "Mommy is here!"

I dropped my things and ran to give Morgan and Conner a hug. My parents followed behind them, and we all met at the top of the porch.

They told me, "Come in and take a look at the place."

Walking in, I was pleasantly surprised.

My parents told me, "We cleaned everything before the movers arrived."

Looking around every room was clean and was an exact match to how our rooms were set up at Mom and Dad's house. The movers still had a few boxes left to bring inside and all of the extra bedroom furniture that we brought from *Pennsylvania*. I had no idea Mom and Dad were going to purchase the same bedroom furniture they had at their house for this house too.

I saw the moving coordinator, and she welcomed me to *Florida*.

She told me, "Whenever you are ready, Please, inspect each room to ensure everything has arrived ok."

I went through each room and everything was in the right place and all of our belongings were there. When I was finished, we had the movers put all the extra furniture from *Pennsylvania* in the storage house. Now the only things left to put away were a few miscellaneous items in boxes on the dining room table.

It was getting late and my parents decided to go home to get some rest.

They said, "We will be back tomorrow to help with anything you need us to do."

Before they left, Mom ordered two large pizzas for us, so I did not have to cook anything. When the pizza arrived, we still had several boxes on the dining room table. We grabbed two crates left in the corner of the dining room and placed the pizza on them as we sat on the floor. We ate and I daydreamed about how much more fulfilled the kid's life were going to be growing up here in *Florida* as I watched them eat.

After the meal, I cleaned up while the kids headed upstairs to get ready for bed. I was exhausted and as soon as I laid my head down on my pillow I was out. I slept for several hours until I had to get up to use the bathroom. I did not want to get up, but I figured I better go ahead. I rolled over to look at the clock and it was 4:03 am.

On my return from the bathroom, a cool breeze passed over my body. I checked all of the windows to see if any were open, but they were all closed and locked. I did not think twice about it, and got back into the bed. I laid there as my mind and thoughts were heavily on Ma Lillie. I ended up having a dream about her when I finally fell back to sleep.

I suddenly woke up and it was 6:33 am. I could not wait to see Mom today so I could tell her about my dream. For the life of me I could not figure out the meaning of the dream. I got up and started putting away the few things left in the boxes on the dining room table. When I finished, I was a little hungry. I opened the freezer door and to my surprise, it was fully stocked to capacity.

Apparently, my parents went grocery shopping before I came because the kitchen cabinets were full of food too. I prepared Conner and Morgan's favorite breakfast, which consisted of sausage links, eggs, and cheese toast. My parents showed up around 8:30 am just after we had finished getting dressed. They were very helpful as we rearranged furniture and took out all of the trash.

After all of that, it was lunchtime. Mom fixed all of us some sandwiches and lemonade. The kids ate then went to play in the yard. Mom and I sat outside on the porch. Dad stayed inside to watch TV.

Mom asked, "How was your first night in your new house?"

I just said, "Ok," at first and wanted to tell her about my dream but decided to wait.

Mom went on to say, "Thank you for deciding to move to *Florida*. The kids have brought us nothing but joy. If you ever need us please do not hesitate to call."

I told Mom, "I love you" and gave her a kiss, which is when I decided to tell her about my dream. I told her, "Mom, I need to tell you something, but I do not want you to think that I am crazy."

Mom said, "Oh baby, you can tell me anything," and gave me a reassuring smile and a hug.

I told her, "I had a dream about Ma Lillie last night."

Mom did not look surprised.

She told me, "Go ahead and tell me about the dream."

I told her, "I saw Ma Lillie in the hallway and she was motioning for me to follow her. I was scared at first, but then I was ok because I knew she would never harm me. She did not speak, but she led me to Conner's room and pointed at the storage closet door in his room. When I opened the door, there was something in the shape of a box inside, but it was not clear what it was. I turned around and she was gone, that is when I woke up."

Mom said, "Hmmm," and asked, "How did she look?"

I told her, "She was wearing a light blue colored nightgown and a pair of white slippers with lilies on them. She had a special glow around her whole body as she seemed to float down the hallway. It felt like she was at peace and happy."

Mom leaned her head back against the chair and closed her eyes and then said, "Just as I remember her, with her favorite nightgown and slippers. Your Grandma always seemed to have a special glow about her."

Mom suddenly opened her eyes and said, "The chest! The chest we found was in the closet in Conner's room in the same location as the box in your dream."

I said, "What chest?" Then I remembered the one we found when we first visited the house. I could not believe I forgot about the chest.

Mom said, "Dad took it and placed it in the garage at home and as far as I know it is still there."

I could only imagine what was inside. I was excited and nervous because it could be a number of different things in the chest.

Mom got up and went inside to find Dad. I followed behind her a few minutes later.

Dad was telling Mom, "The chest is in the garage and it has been there since we found it." He then asked, "Do you want to go see what is inside?"

I immediately said, "Yes," and went to find the kids.

The drive to Mom and Dad's house seemed to be the longest ride ever. The whole way there it was as if I was a little kid looking around and asking, "Are we there yet?" My mind wondered what was so important in that chest that Ma Lillie had to come into my dream to remind me of it.

Dad finally pulled into the driveway and we all hopped out and ran to the garage. I looked at the chest and it was old and dusty. It looked sort of like the ones in the pirate movies. I took a closer look at the lock and realized we had no key to fit it. I inspected the chest a little further and saw an emblem that looked familiar.

I thought back to where I remembered seeing it and then it came to me. There was a small box on top of the fireplace mantle in Ma Lillie's house, with the same emblem on it. I told Mom and Dad about it and said, "The key has to be inside that box."

Dad wanted to smash the chest, but Mom insisted, "We will take it back with us and see if there is a key in the box on the mantle before we destroy it."

Mom told him, "If there is no key in the box on the mantle, I will allow you to smash it or whatever it takes to get it open."

Dad put the chest in the trunk and we hopped back into the car and headed back to *Homestead*. Once we arrived, I ran into the house and straight to the fireplace mantle. The box was exactly where I remembered it. I opened it and just as I thought, there was a key inside along with a note and an envelope. I was shocked to see my name on both the note and envelope. The note stated not to open the envelope until after opening the chest.

I grabbed the key as Dad was bringing in the chest. He sat it down and stepped away. I was so nervous, as I tried to open the lock that my hands began to shake. Mom came over and began to rub my arms and shoulders to help calm me down. I took a deep breath, inserted the key, and turned it. I lifted the top, and it made a loud screeching noise. I was overwhelmed at what I saw, but I thought back to the envelope with my name on it. I grabbed the envelope and began to open it as my heart began to race.

I finally got the envelope open and noticed another key was inside along with another letter. I looked at the letter and realized that it was in Ma Lillie's very own handwriting. It was dated ten years ago, about a year after she had discovered she had cancer.

The letter started with, "My Dearest Meadow. If you are reading this, it means that I have lost my battle with breast cancer and the Lord has taken me to the upper room in the sky. Please do not mourn or feel sorry for me too long for I have had a long and beautiful life."

I read more and could feel the tears welling up in my eyes. I tried to focus on the beautiful words written by Ma Lillie, but it was hard.

She continued the letter by saying, "Meadow you are my only Grandchild, and I Love You dearly. During all of the years I was away from you, I thought of you daily and yearned to hold you in my arms, smell your hair, and to give you lots of kisses. I left my house to your Mother, but I wanted to leave you some of my most precious and unique things to me."

"In the chest, that you have just opened you will see several letters. They were all written by your Grandfather Eddie Thompson. He was a wonderful man who had a special way with words. I put them in the chest for you to read so you can see what the meaning of true love really is. You will also find your Grandpa's Purple Heart and a dog tag from *World War II*. He was shot down by enemy fire, and in the plane crash, he injured his leg."

I picked up the Purple Heart and held it close to my heart. The same way Grandpa Eddie would hold me every time he saw me. I grabbed the dog tag, placed it around my neck, and began to rub my fingertips over the letters of his name. I looked at it and was so proud that he was my Grandpa.

Ma Lillie continued the letter saying, "You will also find several recipes for my pies and cobblers. These particular recipes were passed down to me from my Grandma and have been in the family for several generations. Please follow them carefully, and you too will be able to master the art of making these precious gems and help keep the family tradition alive."

"Finally, you will find a map leading to the tool shed outback indicating another box that can only be opened by the key that was in the envelope containing this letter. Inside the box you will find a pleasant surprise that will change your life."

I took a closer look inside the chest and saw there was a drawing of a family tree, which I drew in 2nd grade. I sent it to Ma Lillie for *Christmas* that same year. I had no idea she had kept it after all of those years.

I also saw two pictures. The first one was just of Ma Lillie and Grandpa Eddie. The second one was of Ma Lillie, Grandpa Eddie, and myself. I was on a tire swing that hung from a *Weeping Willow Tree*. I was smiling and laughing as they both appeared to be pushing me. I remember that day as if it was yesterday and would give anything to be able to see that *Weeping Willow Tree* and swing again.

I grabbed the map, turned to my Mom, and we both had tears in our eyes. We all headed outside toward the tool shed. I looked on the map, and I noticed an X on top of a riding lawnmower. I opened the doors to the shed and looked inside. We saw lots of garden tools and a green *John Deer* riding lawnmower. Dad hopped on the lawnmower, started it up, and began to move it outside the shed. Underneath the lawnmower was a patch of dirt that looked like someone had dug up something.

I grabbed a shovel and started to dig a hole. About a foot later, I saw what looked like a box, and as I brushed off the dirt, it was a box. I opened it with the 2nd key and saw a paper bag with a zip lock bag inside of it and it was full of money. My jaw dropped, and

I said, "Oh my God." We took the money back to the house and began to count it. When we finished, it was a total of $100,000, and it was all in $100 bills. I sat back and said, "Wow. All of this for me?"

Mom said, "Yes for you. It all makes sense now."

I asked Mom what she meant. Her response was that, "Ma Lillie did not like banks or keeping her money in them. Ma Lillie would always save her spare change and dollars in jars until she accumulated enough to make $100, she would then have me take it to the bank, and tell me to exchange it for a crisp $100 bill. Meadow you can only imagine how many times I went to the bank for your Grandma throughout a total of over 25 years, but I had no idea she was saving this money for you the whole time."

CHAPTER 5

Handy Renovations

I sat at the table contemplating what I should do with all of this money. I told my parents, "I cannot possibly keep all of this for myself. I am going to give some of it to you guys."

Both parents simultaneously responded with a resounding, "No!"

Mom said, "The money belongs to you. Your Grandma saved it and left it for you, not us. We cannot accept any of it."

I said, "Ok," and left the room to look for a bag to put the money in, but I was still not sure what I was going to do with it. I found a duffle bag that all of the money would fit in nicely then put it in my closet in the bedroom.

I did not get a lot of sleep that night because I was trying to digest what happened earlier in the day and how much the money meant even more stability for me and the kids.

The next morning, the kids and I went to *Wal-Mart*. We walked around and I thought about what to do with the extra furniture we had from *Pennsylvania*. I told the kids, "You know, we could have a yard sale this weekend to try to sell the extra furniture and the money we make could be split between both of you."

They both cheered as we headed to the hardware section to look for yard sale signs. I called Mom and Dad to tell them my idea and to ask if they had anything, they wanted to donate. I figured they would because yard sales were one of their many loves.

They said, "That is a good idea and we have several items that we can contribute to your cause to help you out."

I started going through my purse looking for a pen when I came across a piece of paper with a list of ingredients for Ma Lillie's pies that I had written down the other day.

Since I was in the store, I decided to go ahead and buy the items needed to start making them. I walked through the spice aisle looking for cinnamon and I thought back to that attractively gorgeous man I met named Dylan. I closed my eyes and said, "Umm," as I imagined his naked body all over me. I quickly opened my eyes and said, "I need to call him." I finished getting everything I needed and we headed to the counter.

It was late afternoon and on the way home, I decided to ride around to try to get familiar with the town. One place we rode by was the school where the kids were going to be attending. We noticed some kids having football practice and some cheerleaders nearby. Conner and Morgan got excited, and I told them, "I will sign you up soon." We arrived back to the house, and the kids hopped out of the car and as usual ran to the tire swing. I unpacked the bags and began to walk through the house to see if I could find anything that we did not need any more so we could add it to the yard sale this weekend.

I headed back to the kitchen to put away the groceries and to start on dinner. I prepared *Cornish Hens* for baking and then I started on the baked potatoes and the mac and cheese. While waiting for the food to finish cooking, I began to read the local newspaper. I saw some coupons for pie crusts, which reminded me of Ma Lillie's recipes again. I went to my bedroom and looked on my dresser.

There were several recipes to choose from that included apple pie, peach cobbler, sweet potato pie, blackberry cobbler, and a pecan pie. I decided that the apple pie was going to be the first one I would bake. I followed the recipe exactly how Ma Lillie had written it out. When the pie was finished baking, I took it out of the oven and sat it on the counter, so it could cool before slicing it.

Dylan was heavily on my mind again. I grabbed my bag and got his phone number. I was nervous and paused a few times before ultimately dialing his number. A part of me did not want him to answer, and another part of me did.

After the third ring, he answered. I hesitated a few seconds before I said, "Hello Dylan, this is Meadow. I hope you remember me."

Dylan's response was, "Of course I remember you. I have been eagerly awaiting your call."

I said, "Ok great," and I apologized for the length of time it took me to call him back. I explained how busy I have been with the move and getting things situated in the house.

Dylan said, "It is ok, my Pop Warner Football team has only had two practices so far." He continued to say, "I have a spot for Conner on the team, and a spot is also available for Morgan if she is interested in cheerleading, but I was just waiting for your call."

I said, "Great, because I am ready to sign both of them up."

Dylan said, "Fantastic, I will register them first thing tomorrow morning." He then asked, "What is your email address? so I can send you the forms."

We continued to talk as I filled out the forms, scanned them, and emailed them back to him. I mentioned to him, "We are going to have a yard sale this weekend."

Dylan said, "Well, maybe I will come by to see you."

I was excited to hear he wanted to see me. I told him, "I would love that," and did not hesitate to give him my address and the time for the yard sale.

Dylan said, "Ok, I will see you then."

I hung up and noticed my arm glistening with sweat. I had to walk over and stand in front of the fan just to cool off.

The kids came in from playing and they were hungry. I sent them off to wash their hands while I fixed their plates. After finishing our meal, I told the kids, "I have a surprise for you!"

They were excited and jumped up and down while asking, "What is it?"

I grabbed the apple pie and said, "Dessert!" I was nervous because I did not know how it would taste. I prayed the kids would like it. They both took a bite but did not respond immediately.

I started to worry, then both of them said, "It tastes really good Mom. Can we have another slice?"

I breathed a sigh of relief as I took a bite myself. I was impressed, and it did taste pretty good. It made me proud to know that I could continue my family's tradition for another generation.

I began to clear the table and wash the dishes. The kids started to talk about how excited they were about the yard sale coming up and what they were going to buy with their money. I laughed to myself as they argued about how much money they were going to make.

Conner suggested, "We should serve the customers complimentary lemonade for appreciation and sell slices of pie and cobbler."

I said, "That is a superb idea. We can have the yard sale setup near the road and use Ma Lillie's old fruit and vegetable stand for the complimentary lemonade and to sell the slices of pie and cobbler."

The next morning, we got up and headed back to the store to get more ingredients and supplies. The rest of the day was spent baking pies and cobblers, rolling lemons, and stirring lemonade.

Later, that night the kids were worn out so they headed upstairs to turn in for the night. I went into the living room and sat on the couch. I turned on the television and stretched out to relax. I woke up with Morgan hovered over me playing with my eyelids. It was daylight already, and both kids were already showered and dressed. The television was still on the same channel I was watching before falling asleep. I sat up and began to rub my eyes.

Suddenly, the doorbell rang. I got up and walked towards the door, and could smell the aroma of the pies and cobblers from the kitchen. I pondered who was at the door then asked, "Who is it?"

The reply was, "Mom and Dad!"

They came in, kissed me on the cheek then ran to embrace the kids.

Dad said, "I am going to unload all the stuff that we brought and then I will get the stuff out of the storage house."

I went to take a shower and my mind flashed back to Dylan and his tight muscular body and his handsome innocent face. The water began to drizzle down my body as I leaned my back against the wall. A tingly sensation of sexual energy began to travel from my nipples down through my spine and nosedived straight for my clit. I opened my legs and maneuvered my body to allow the warm, tantalizing water to drizzle down directly onto my clit.

The water got my body so hot that steam began to simultaneously come from my skin and fog up the glass door. My clit and vagina began to pulsate like a heartbeat between my legs.

I slowly slid my fingers inside of my vagina and began to masturbate as I had done so many times before, but this time was different. I started to moan softly to myself then suddenly there was a knock on the bathroom door. My mind went blank and back to reality.

It was my Mother on the other side of the door asking, "Are you ok?" and "How much longer are you going to be?"

I told her, "I will be down soon." I finally finished dressing and came down stairs. No one was inside the house, so I proceeded to head outdoors. I opened the front door, and to my amazement, I noticed several cars parked on the side of the road, with about eight people walking around sipping on lemonade, eating pie, cobbler, and looking through all of the items for sale.

I made my way to the fruit stand and met Morgan halfway yelling, "Look Mommy look!" as she was carrying a tip jar full of change that she was jingling.

I asked, "What do we have here?"

Morgan responded, "I am rich."

I laughed and said, "That is great baby."

Walking up to where all of the items for sale were, I saw Mom and Dad being the experienced yard salespersons as usual. They were, engaged with two different couples and making sales. More than half of the items were already gone, and Dad had a pocket full of money in his smock. Connor was inside the fruit stand selling slices of pie and cobbler, collecting money, and pouring lemonade. He was definitely a young hustler.

The last few customers began to leave as we suddenly heard a loud rumbling noise from a truck coming up the road. It started to slow down and pulled over near the booth. To my surprise, it was Dylan.

He got out and had his daughter Casey with him. I wanted to run and jump into his arms, but I somehow composed myself and went to greet them. Dylan introduced me to Casey, and I commented on how beautiful she was. I thanked them for coming and called over my parents and the kids.

I told them, "This is my friend Dylan, the Pop Warner Football coach I met in the grocery store, and his lovely daughter Casey." My mom gave me a big smile and winked at me after greeting Dylan and Casey with a big hug.

Conner and Morgan immediately greeted them and asked, "Do you want some lemonade and a slice of pie or cobbler?"

Dylan and Casey both said, "Sure."

Conner told him, "Your total is $2.00," as he went to ring him up on the cash register.

Dylan pulled out a $5.00 bill and smiled as he said, "Keep the change."

Dylan and I looked into each other's eyes and smiled.

Morgan grabbed Casey by the hand after she finished her slice of pie and they took off in a full sprint toward the tire swing with Conner trailing close behind them. I told Dylan, "Let me show you around."

He said, "Sure, there might be something I would like to buy."

I said, "There are only a few things left," and made our way over to the items.

Dylan's attention immediately was drawn to the two beds and he asked, "How much do you want for them?"

My Dad said, "For you $100."

Dylan said, "Ok, but I will give you $200." He stated, "My daughter needs a new bed and the extra bed I will put in the guest room."

My Dad shook his hand and told him, "You have a deal!"

Dylan and my Dad took the two beds and put them on the back of his truck and strapped them down while I supervised.

Afterward, I took Dylan on a tour of the land and we settled down to take a break on the swing overlooking the pond. We laughed and joked as we flirted with each other through our eyes.

Dylan asked me, "What are you interested in? What do you like to do for fun?"

I told him, "I am into painting and art." I went on to say, "I have an area in the house that I would like to one-day convert into an art studio, but I need to find a contractor to do the work."

Dylan said, "That sounds cool, and I would love to see this room."

I was shocked that he was interested and said, "Ok, let's go now if you have time."

Dylan said, "I have plenty of time," and we proceeded to the house.

On the way, we saw my parents gathering the last few items that were left so they could put them back in the storage house. The kids were still busy playing in the yard.

Dylan was very interested in the house and even began to describe what type of columns were on the porch. He explained everything about the house from the design of the ceiling to what types of windows and doors were in the house. I took him to the room that I wanted to transform into my art studio. I told him, "This area was used as Ma Lillie's store area." Dylan began to describe all the possibilities and even gave me an estimate of what it would cost. I was amazed and asked, "How do you know so much about houses?"

Dylan responded by saying, "I went to school for a couple of years for Structural Engineering but had to drop out. My Dad also use to be a builder, so I have been around it all my life."

He reached into his pocket, pulled out his wallet, and handed me a business card. I looked at it, and it read, "Dylan's Renovations."

Dylan explained, "I am a contractor who does renovations and additions to houses."

Then he showed me on his cell phone pictures of his most recent work. I was shocked because I had no idea.

Dylan said, "Let me know when you want me to start. I have a whole crew. A person to draw and design the layout and even a person that could build a small-scale model of the renovation."

I told him, "I will be ready in a few weeks after the kids, and I get settled."

Dylan said, "ok."

It was getting late, so we called for Casey and headed toward Dylan's truck. I thanked him again for coming and told him, "I really enjoyed your company." I wrapped my arms around his neck and gave him a hug and we both agreed to see each other again.

The kids said goodbye to Casey, and we watched as his truck disappeared up the road.

When we got back to the house, Dad was watching tv and Mom had just finished preparing some food for us. We washed our hands, and we all sat down to enjoy our meal. Mom and Dad were very pleased with the outcome of the yard sale.

Morgan quickly asked, "How much money did we make?"

Dad said, "We have not counted it yet. I wanted all of us to do it together."

We all finished eating, cleaned off the table, and washed the dishes. Dad brought in all the money including the jar full of change, and we spread it over the table. We all started to count the money and came to a final total of $836.38.

Conner asked, "How much of it is mine?"

I told him, "$418.19." They jumped up and did their little happy dance.

Mom and Dad told them, "Do not spend it all in one place."

The next few weeks Dylan and I saw each other several times. We did not go on any dates but we just spent quality time talking and learning more about each other. I finally got to a point that I felt it was time to start working on my vision for the art studio. The kids had settled into their new school and had begun to make new friends. Now it was time for me to get back to my passion.

A few days later while we were going for a walk at a local park, I told Dylan, "I am ready to go ahead with my art studio project." The next day Dylan showed up early and began to take measurements of the room.

He did not stay long, but said, "I will be back."

When he returned; he had a truck fully loaded with building supplies.

He unloaded the supplies and then said, "I will see you in the morning."

The next morning Dylan showed up with his crew and had a printed layout of the new design that contained everything we had discussed over the last few weeks. By the end of that day, all of the framing for the walls were complete, and they were ready for sheet rocking, which they finished the next day.

Dylan told me, "The room is ready to be painted and said we should paint it together since painting is your love and passion."

I said, "Ok," and was so excited that I did not sleep at all that night.

CHAPTER 6

Strokes of Paint

Dylan came to the house the next morning around 8:30 am. I had just gotten back from *Panera Bread* with a *Caffe latte*, coffee, and some bagels. We both sat down at the table and ate, while flirting with each other the whole time. Afterward, I cleaned up the table while Dylan went into the bathroom to change into his painter's coveralls. He came out smiling at me as he proceeded to head to the Art Studio area. I went upstairs so I could change into my coveralls.

In the meantime, he began to cover up the floor of the room. When I came back downstairs and entered the Art Studio Dylan's back was toward me. I quietly grabbed a paintbrush, dipped it into some paint, and flung the paint from the brush at him. The paint landed all over the back of his coveralls, and some even got in his hair.

I laughed as he tried to figure out what happened. He turned around and started laughing as well.

He told me, "This means war!"

Then grabbed his paintbrush, dipped it into the paint bucket and began to chase me around the room slinging paint everywhere.

After a while I was tired of running, so I started to climb up the 8-foot tall ladder in the middle of the room. I only made it up a few steps before Dylan grabbed me around the waist. I turned around with paint all over my face and smiled at him as I sat down on one of the steps.

He looked at me as he stood on the floor and he said, "Now it is time to unleash the dragon!"

The comment turned me on, and I calmly said, "Take me Daddy!" and he did. It started with a kiss that made me feel the passion in his lips explode through my body. It was like a magical electrical current, up and down my spine seemingly exploding through my nipples and the tip of my clit. It felt so good I could feel my juices uncontrollably oozing out of me and slowly creeping down my thighs.

Where I was sitting on the ladder, I was about eye level to Dylan's chest. I purposely moved down a couple of steps, so I was mouth level with his dick. Reaching out I grabbed the zipper to his coveralls, which were covered in paint and began to unzip them.

Together we peeled them off his massive chest and arms. I was pleasantly surprised because he was totally naked underneath. I ran into problems trying to get the rest of the coveralls off, so we both began to tear and rip them until they fell to the floor.

Finally, there he stood butt ass naked and all I could say was, "Thank you, Jesus!" I was so in awe that I did not know where to start on his body, but I figured it out. I began to lick his chest and nipples while I grabbed his huge ass dick. It was rock hard as I held it in my hand and could feel it throbbing as I stroked it. Immediately, my pussy started to pulsate and yearn for his dick to pleasure my insides. It had been ten long years since I had been with a man.

I made my way down his chest with my tongue. The temptation of tasting his dick made my mouth water as I yearned for his long hot rod to enter my mouth. I started to lick around his head to tease him a bit before I wrapped my lips around it. I began to deep throat it, devouring every inch. I continued sucking his dick for a few minutes until he began to moan with such intensity that I could tell he was going to be cumming soon.

I was not ready for him to cum yet, but if he did, I was prepared to swallow every drip drop of it. I wanted him to tattoo my inner walls and then polish them walls with all of his liquid passion.

Dylan grabbed his hammer from his tool belt and used it to unzip my coveralls. To his amazement, all I had on underneath was a tennis skirt and a sports bra. I removed my shoes and my coveralls dropped down the ladder onto the floor directly on top of his coveralls. My hair was in two ponytails and I was looking like a teenage high school cheerleader.

My body started to rise off the ladder as he licked my stomach, which was tight, toned, and well defined from all the Pilates workouts I had done over the past ten years. I had to hide it from my ex-husband Steve because he would have said that it looked manly and unattractive.

I enjoyed the body washing Dylan gave me with his tongue, but I was so ready to feel that dick deep inside me. I turned over on my stomach and held onto the sides of the ladder to give him his final surprise.

Dylan lifted up my skirt, and all he could see was my ass and my hairy pussy from the back. He smiled as he stuck his finger inside. It was like he was trying to measure how wet and deep my pussy was. I could hear my juices start to gush all over his finger as he slid it in and out of me. The deeper Dylan went inside my vagina, the deeper the arch in my back became, allowing him to slide his thumb even deeper inside me. At this point I was moaning intensely.

After he finished stroking me with his thumb from behind, he pulled it out and stared at me with his intense blue eyes. He then started to lick my cum off of his thumb. It turned me on so much that I grabbed his hand and joined him in licking and began to suck his thumb like a baby. When I finished, there was not one drop of cum left on any part of his thumb.

Dylan started to climb up the ladder behind me as I moved up about two steps. He ended up standing on the bottom step. I leaned forward and laid against the ladder for balance as I reached back and flipped up my skirt. I grabbed both of my cheeks and spread them as wide as I could get them while laying my head down on one of the steps.

Dylan mounted me and gently slid his massive rod up inside me pushing it all the way in and slowly taking it out. He repeated this about three to four times before he put it all the way in and just left it there.

It was like Dylan wanted it to marinate inside me. I repeatedly whispered, "Fuck me!" until he started to stroke my pussy like it was no tomorrow or if it was going to be the last time, I was going to give it to him. I grabbed the sides of the ladder tighter and held on for dear life. With every stroke, it felt as if his cock grew thicker and longer. I showed my gratitude by pushing down as he was stroking up and I moaned as I came all over his dick multiple times.

Dylan continuously stroked my wet and creamy white pussy until it began to talk to him. She was repeatedly telling him, "Thank you over and over again." After about another hour of slow, deep, and intense thrusting, Dylan unloaded his warm load up inside of me. Thank God I had an IUD.

I immediately suggested that we go upstairs because I wanted more of what he was so willing to give, and what I was so ready to receive. I was lying face down on the steps of the ladder trying to savor every moment of the pleasure I just received. It took a few minutes but I finally managed to muster up enough energy to climb down.

All of a sudden, I heard a loud smacking sound and felt this sharp sensation run from my left ass cheek through the rest of my body. Apparently, Dylan had stuck his hand in some paint and spanked my ass as hard as he could. I felt the remains of some wetness on my cheek. I turned to look at my ass and I could see his handprint. I loved it and it just made me stick my ass out a little further so he could spank my right cheek as well, because I like my pleasure spread evenly.

After rubbing my clit several times, I finally climbed down the ladder and we cleaned ourselves up as good as we could without a shower. I started upstairs with Dylan close behind me. About half way up I felt him grab my right ankle. I turned around to see what he was doing, and felt his soft wet tongue slowly making its way up the back of my heel and up my leg. It ignited my fire all over again.

He continued licking up my leg until he reached the bottom of my ass cheeks, which were sticking out of the back of the tennis skirt. Grabbing the sides of my waist he slowly began to peel my tennis skirt off my body. After getting it about halfway down my legs, he grabbed my cheeks and spread them as he took his tongue and began to lick my pussy from the back.

It felt so good that I took off my sports bra and started fondling my breasts and nipples. I slowly closed my eyes and braced myself as he made his way to my clit. He licked and sucked on it until I began to cum all over his tongue.

His dick began to rise and throb against my leg. The sudden rush of blood down south must have made him temporarily black out. He paused and shook his head before he continued massaging my clit with his tongue. The more he licked, the more his dick throbbed against my leg.

After several minutes, I could not take it anymore. I turned over on my back and told him, "Fuck this pussy!" Without hesitation, he slid all of his manhood inside of me. It was so wet that it started to make smacking noises again.

Unexpectedly, he pulled out and started looking at his dick. I guess he could not believe how wet I was so he had to see for himself. After wiping some of my wetness off with his finger, he placed it on my lip as I slowly opened my mouth and fooled him into thinking I was going to lick his finger.

Instead, I turned around, positioned myself securely on one of the steps, grabbed his dick and started licking away my very own pussy juice, from his balls all the way up the back spine of his shaft until I reached the tip of his head.

While I was doing this, I stared up at him with my fuck me eyes. This drove him wild. I quickly turned around, and allowed Dylan to slip back up inside me and he began to once again stroke my pussy. I assisted him by pumping back and it was as if we were on a seesaw or playing tug of war with his dick and my pussy. I was cumming the whole time.

Suddenly, I let out a moan that seemed to never end. When I stopped moaning, it was a relief, as my body just shut down, and my legs started to go into convulsions trembling out of control as he pulled out and came all over me. Trust me there were no walls painted in that room that day. I was so exhausted that I went to sleep right there on the steps.

I woke up on the couch with my favorite Leopard blanket draped over me. Dylan was gone. I did wonder where he was but sleep seemed more important at the time. I grabbed my blanket, wrapped up tight, and fell back to sleep. When I woke up later that night, I went upstairs. Walking by my bed, I noticed a sheet of paper with something written on it lying in the middle of the bed. I picked it up and began to read.

Hello Beautiful,

Sorry, I had to leave so soon. I did not want to wake you while you were sleeping so peacefully, so I left you this letter. The more time I spend with you, the more you captivate me with your mind, body, and spirit. I wanted you to know that making love to you was magical! It was like time stopped, and only you and I existed in the whole entire world. It felt as if our bodies merged into one and I could feel your spirit run through my soul!

Dylan

My heart fluttered as I laid back on the bed. I placed the poem against my chest as I let out a sigh of relief. About an hour later Dylan called. We talked about how spending the day together felt so free. I told him, "It was like enjoying nature, going camping, or like a day at the beach."

Dylan told me, "I love the beach and camping."

We ended up talking on the phone until the sun came up that next morning.

CHAPTER 7

Ocean's 2012

The next few weeks were spent putting the final touches on my art studio space. After all of the walls were finally painted, we started moving in the equipment and art supplies. I was not sure of what I would use the art studio for besides a therapeutic peace of mind.

I did know that my first project was going to be the mural painting of the landscape overlooking the coffee shop window in *Scranton, PA*. I loved that view, and it brightened my day every morning after I would drop off the kids at school. I wanted it to be the first thing I would see every time I came in the house.

Dylan and I began to make plans for a trip to the beach, but we did not just want to go to the beach, we also wanted to go camping at a nearby campsite.

Our plan was to spend a whole weekend together. Leave on a Friday afternoon, and return Sunday night. Connor and Morgan were going to be with Mom and Dad, and Casey was going to stay over a friend's house.

We wanted to do things a little different and stray away from the traditional way of camping. We decided to go to *Wal-Mart* and instead of buying sleeping bags, we purchased an airbed. Instead of hamburgers and hot dogs, we bought steaks, baking potatoes, two whole ears of corn, and ingredients needed to make a homemade pizza. It had been a long time since either of us had been camping, so we wanted to make it as enjoyable and romantic as we could.

Midday Friday, Mom and Dad came to pick up the kids. Dylan dropped Casey at her friend's house, and then came to my house.

We packed everything in the back of his truck and started on our journey.

Looking at the GPS, it was going to take about 45 minutes to get there. The sun was shining, and the sky was a bright blue. All of the clouds in the sky looked like giant floating cotton balls. I rolled the window down, so I could feel the cool refreshing breeze blow through my hair.

Dylan was trying to find a radio station. Suddenly, he found one that played classic rock n roll songs all day. The song playing at the time was "*I Love Rock N Roll,*" by *Joan Jett & the Blackhearts.* We both began to sing the words and acted as if we were members of the band. Dylan was on the drums, and I was on the guitar. We sang and laughed through each song that came on until we reached the campground. We checked in at the registration station and then rode around in search of our campsite.

Dylan said, "Here we are, campsite #231, home for the next few days."

Dylan grabbed the tent and began to set it up. I started taking the camping supplies out of the truck and placed them on the picnic table.

In the distance, we began to hear rumblings of thunder but thought nothing of it because the sun was still shining bright. A short time later as Dylan nailed in the last peg for the tent, it began to pour down raining. Everyone at the campsite was shocked and started to panic and scramble for shelter.

Dylan grabbed one of the tarps that we had just bought and began to cover the tent. I quickly moved everything inside to prevent them from getting wet. Dylan had some rope, but it was not enough to secure the tarp to the trees as needed to keep the rain from soaking the tent.

I asked him, "Can I help?"

He told me, "Go inside, and I will take care of it."

Dylan saw a tree nearby that had a fishing line tied around it from what looked like a make shift clothesline left from previous campers. He quickly cut the line and used it to secure the tarp so it would not blow away in the wind.

The whole time it felt as if we were in the middle of a monsoon. At one point the rain began to blow sideways. Dylan was soaking wet, I was soaking wet, and the majority of our things inside the tent were wet in some kind of way.

Dylan finally came inside and took off his wet t-shirt. His chest was wet and glistening as droplets of water ran down his body. He looked as if he had rubbed himself down in oil for a bodybuilding competition. My shirt was soaking wet, and I looked as if I was about to enter a wet t-shirt contest. I had on no bra, and my nipples were hard and exposed through my shirt. I commented, "The rain turns me on."

Dylan said, "Doing the nasty in the rain has always been a fantasy of mine."

He walked away slowly and partially pulled down his soaking wet shorts. I did not see any underwear, so I asked, "Do you have on any underwear?"

He smiled and said, "No," and stated, "I never wear underwear! They are too confining."

I stared as his huge dick began to rise, which helped prevent his shorts from falling to the floor. I gladly reached down to help expose *Luke Skywalker* and started to play with him in my hand. I could not help myself, so I dropped to my knees and began to lick the bottom of his dick, then around the top of it. Dylan stood above me with both hands on his hips, as if he was a king or the superhero *Thor*.

I slid *Luke Skywalker* deeper into my mouth and slowly began to wrap my lips and tongue around it. I moved up and down on it repeatedly, as I gazed into his deep blue eyes. It turned me on so much that I reached down into my panties, and began to play with my clit. I slurped up and down on his stiff hard dick for several minutes until he could not take any more. He pulled his dick out of my mouth and started to spew his nut everywhere. I said, "No, please share!" I then latched back onto his dick and finished him off.

The rain had slowed to the point where it was just a drizzle. The dark storm clouds and the abundance of trees made the campsite pitch black. I grabbed Dylan by the hand and headed outside. He was naked and somehow my shorts and panties made their way to my knees. I guided him over to the picnic table where he pulled my shorts and panties all the way off, freeing me to spread my legs as wide as I could get them.

He bent me over the table and began to lick me from behind while playing with my clit at the same time. His tongue felt like a slightly melted ice cube every time he licked me. It added to the already chilly breeze that was blowing on my whole entire body. I instantly began to cream all over his tongue. There was a brief pause from him licking then suddenly, I could feel his dick part my pussy lips and make its way inside my vagina.

The rain was bouncing and sliding down the middle of my back. My breasts were shaking uncontrollably inside my soaking wet shirt. My nipples were standing erect and getting more stimulated as they repeatedly rubbed against the inside of my shirt.

Unexpectedly, Dylan pulled his dick out and began to skeet all over my ass cheeks. I looked back and could see all of his soldiers washing away in the rain.

We went back inside the tent and dried off as we waited for the airbed to finish blowing up. Somehow, we managed to find some dry clothes; then we went to take a shower. The rest of the night we spent cuddled up enjoying each other's body heat along with the view of the moon and the stars.

We woke up the next day and, it was like a sauna inside the tent. Dylan unzipped the door and it was bright and sunny with no sign of any clouds in the sky. The ground was soaking wet with puddles of water everywhere.

We got up and began to gather all of our clothing that were wet and took them to the laundry house and placed them in the dryer. While the clothes were drying, we went to the bathhouse to take a shower. After I had finished showering, I headed back to the laundry house and began to fold our clothes. Dylan joined a few minutes later to help. When we finished, we gathered everything and headed back to the tent.

Dylan started unpacking his propane stovetop and then began to prepare some breakfast for us. When he was finished, we sat down and enjoyed a sausage, egg, and cheese omelet with hash browns and apple juice. We started to have a conversation about what we wanted to do today. The first thing we knew we had to do was go shopping for some swimwear.

About an hour later we made our way out of the campground and headed north up the strip. There were stores on every corner selling everything from swimwear to jewelry. We ended up stopping at an outlet store called *Eagles*. It had an arcade, ice cream parlor, and a fast food restaurant inside.

We walked around, and I playfully teased Dylan by pointing out particular bikinis that would be very revealing or too small for me. I finally found one that I liked that fit me perfectly and headed to the counter to purchase it. Dylan made his way to the men's section where he quickly found a pair of swimming trunks he liked and joined me in line. I grabbed his trunks and placed them on the counter with the rest of my stuff, but it was really only one thing I wanted to grab but I refrained from doing so in such a public place.

Dylan saw some sunglasses as we were waiting to be checked out and we both grabbed a pair. After I had paid for everything, Dylan grabbed the bag and threw me the keys to his truck, as he made his way to the passenger side. I was surprised but gladly grabbed them and hopped in the driver seat. I turned the key and could instantly feel the power of the roaring engine. The vibration started at my toes, made its way up my leg, and made a circular motion as it passed throughout my whole body. I got that sensation every time I pushed the gas pedal. It was just like having a thousand-pound vibrator at my services. I leaned my head towards the window and let the wind blow through my hair, as I enjoyed the cool sensation of the breeze and the vibrations radiating throughout my body.

Dylan placed his hand on my leg and began to rub it softly, mimicking the throwing of a rock or pebble into a body of water. I could feel the ripples start from the center and radiate outward throughout my skin. Those ripples headed up my leg and straight to my clit. I did not want to stop driving, and I could have driven up and down that strip the rest of the day. I am not sure how we made it back to the campground in one piece with all of the times I closed my eyes and laid my head back against the headrest, but we did.

When we arrived back to the campsite my panties were soaking wet and my legs were weak. We changed clothes, gathered our snacks, beach chairs, umbrella, alcoholic beverages, and a mat. We then made our way down the 300ft long pathway to the beach. It was hot but with a cool breeze coming off the water.

Dylan started setting up the umbrella, and I set up the mat and beach chairs underneath it. We sat down and started to enjoy the sounds of the waves. The Seagulls were flying above, and all different types of people of all races were walking by. It was so relaxing and peaceful.

I asked Dylan, "Do you want your snack?" as I reached for the bag. I grabbed his *Zebra Cakes* and handed them to him as he walked over to our mini cooler. He got out a *Corona* for him and a wine cooler for me. There was a sign posted that stated, "*No alcoholic beverages allowed on the beach*," so we carefully poured our drinks as planned earlier into our plastic containers. We sat, laughed, and talked about everyone who walked by.

After finishing our snack, Dylan got up and said, "I will race you to the water." Before I could even say, "Ok," he took off towards the ocean and had a big lead on me. He reached the water first but instantly came to a sudden stop because the water was colder than he had anticipated.

I laughed and said, "That is what you get for cheating!" I then playfully splashed water in his face. He grabbed me, hugged me, and then gave me a kiss just before we were hit by a big wave that knocked both of us over.

We played in the water for a little while then decided to take a walk along the beach. Holding hands, we occasionally stopped to collect unique looking seashells. Suddenly, we continuously started to see several dead jellyfish washed up on the sand. I started to get emotional because of my love for all animals. My eyes began to tear up as I said a short prayer for them with hopes that they had a soul and would go to heaven.

After returning to our spot on the beach, we decided to sit down at the edge of the water with our toes in the sand. We just talked and enjoyed each other's company, but had to keep moving back occasionally because the tide had begun to rise. By now, it was getting late in the evening, and most of the people had left the beach and headed back to the campgrounds.

Around 7:00 pm we gathered all of our stuff and headed back to the campsite. It had begun to get dark, so we took out the lanterns, hung one on a pole to light the area outside the tent, and placed the other directly on the picnic table. This one would be for our lantern lit dinner we were about to prepare.

We unpacked the steaks, baked potatoes, and fresh corn on the cob. I grabbed the potatoes and corn then started to prepare them to be placed on the hot coals. Dylan grabbed some firewood he had on the back of the truck and put them in the fire pit along with some charcoal. He soaked them in lighter fluid and set them ablaze. I waited a few minutes to allow the fire to die down and to give the coals a little time to get hotter. When they were ready, I placed the potatoes and the corn both wrapped in aluminum foil directly on the hot coals, turning them every so often to ensure they were completely done throughout and not just one side.

Dylan had prepared the steaks, and placed them on the grill. They were about halfway done when I gathered a head of lettuce, tomatoes, cucumbers, croutons, shredded cheese, and began to make a salad. When I finished, I went to check on the corn and the potatoes which were almost ready but needed a few more minutes.

I walked up on Dylan and hugged him from behind as I began to fondle *Luke Skywalker*. I whispered in his ear, "I want to cum on it." Dylan smiled and leaned his head back. I walked away and headed toward the tent. Before I went inside, I turned and looked back at him with my fuck me eyes, then disappeared inside the tent but not before flashing my breasts to him.

When I came back out, the steaks were ready to be served. Dylan was checking the corn and the potatoes. I got the plates and placed one on each side of the picnic table with forks, knives, and wine glasses. I grabbed the bowl of salad and the bottle of wine that had been chilling on ice.

We sat down and I poured us some wine. Dylan blessed the food with a prayer. We passed around the food and fixed our own plates then began to eat. Everything was so good that we did not speak at all for a few minutes because we were so busy stuffing our faces.

After a few bites I asked Dylan, "What is your definition of family?" and "What does family mean to you?"

He paused only to finish chewing what was in his mouth then looked into my eyes and began to say, "Family is a lifetime commitment of love, and family is, being there for your loved ones through the thick and thin. Family is also having someone to depend on when everything in the world just goes so wrong, and life turns its back on you. Family is someone holding your hand and telling you it will be ok. Family is standing beside someone when you know they have done wrong, embarrassed, and hurt the family name, but you stand by them regardless."

He then grabbed my hands and said, "Family is having someone worth dying for, just because you want them to have a chance or opportunity at a better life than you had."

I could just feel the passion in Dylan's voice as he spoke. I looked into his eyes and embraced his fire, and knew at that moment; I had found my special someone.

We were both stuffed from the meal, so we went inside. Dylan had some neon glow sticks that he placed along the top mesh part of the tent, and took a few and made them into a neon glowstick disco ball, which Dylan hung from the center of the tent. We both lay on the airbed gazing up at the stars. The tent being lit up with neon lights reminded me of *Christmas*.

Outside the tent we could hear some other campers walking by from time to time. One of them was a little boy, and his Dad.

The little boy said, "Wow, Dad look at the space ship tent!"

It was because of all the neon lights at the top of the tent that were visible from the outside. We both laughed about it then Dylan cuddled up behind me and gently kissed me on the back of my neck. We were in the middle of the woods in a tent, but I had never felt safer than I did that night, with his big biceps wrapped around me so tight.

A few hours later, I woke up still in his arms. Apparently, we both drifted off to sleep, and now it was about 11:00 pm. Both of us were refreshed and energized from the nap. We decided to go for a walk on the beach to enjoy the romantic sound of the crashing waves and the cool breeze blowing off the ocean. Both of us gathered a blanket, flashlight, and a rolled-up mat.

On the way to the beachfront, we passed groups of people on their way back to the campsite, which left only a few individuals out on the beach searching for seashells and Hermit crabs. We walked for a while until we found a perfect spot high on top of one of the sand dunes. I spread out the mat, and we both sat and watched the high tide from the light of the moon and the stars. Dylan got the blanket, wrapped it around me, and I leaned my head on his shoulder.

About 30 minutes later everyone seemed to disappear off the beach, and it was just Dylan, the ocean, and myself. Dylan suddenly stood up and said he would be right back. He removed his swimming trunks, and I wondered what he was doing, but was glad to be a witness to his naked body once again. I did not know if Dylan wanted me to suck his dick, to fuck me, or what, but I got excited.

He clearly had other plans. I could only laugh as I had to quickly process what was happening. All I could see was this tightly toned man with his two tight ass cheeks in motion running towards the ocean.

He dove in just as a wave was approaching and disappeared for a few seconds. All of a sudden Dylan rose out of the water as if he was on a secret mission as a member of the *Navy Seals*. He motioned for me to join him.

I stood up without hesitation, threw off my bikini and ran as fast as I could towards him in the water. He grabbed my naked body as I jumped into his arms and he twirled me around. He sat me down in the water as a wave came and splashed all over my body, which had not adjusted to the temperature of the water, so it was a little shocking.

Dylan kissed me on my neck as he began to finger me in the water. I led him out of the water and onto the edge of the sand. I got down on my knees in the doggy style position with him behind me. He started to play with my clit as the water splashed up against it. I wanted him so bad that I leaned forward with my ass in the air and placed my forehead in the sand.

Dylan slowly started to kiss up the back of my legs and planted his face between my ass cheeks. He licked and sucked on my clit. Dylan's tongue was warm, the water from the ocean was cool. Both of them combined caused my body to quiver. I turned my head to look between my legs and noticed him stroking his hard dick while he was eating my pussy.

After cumming multiple times, I grabbed his dick, and slowly slid it into my creamy wet vagina.

It was as if we had died and gone to heaven as I saw a bright light from above. It turned out to be a plane flying over us. Apparently, there was an airport less than a half mile from the beach. Dylan did not stop and even grabbed a handful of my hair as he continued to stroke, and thrust his grade "A" beef deep inside me.

All I could do was try to grip the sand. I could hear a constant smacking noise from the wetness of my pussy, and the sound of wet flesh banging against each other.

He grabbed me by the waist and began to pull me back towards him as he thrust forward. My tits were flopping back and forth, and they were totally stimulated from the cool air and sand. They began to clap and high five each other like two hands.

Dylan began to give me a massage, while he fucked me from behind. Rubbing his massive hands up the middle of my spine and down the sides of my back. I was in the doggy style position with a slight arch in my back, which I used to proposition him to go deeper. With every deep stroke I would gasp for air and thank the Lord at the same time.

He was close to cumming because his already hard dick began to get harder. I was so ready for his hot load to warm my back. He grabbed my hips and gave me a few last strokes then pulled out and began to skeet all over my back.

I rubbed in as much as I could before a wave came and washed the rest away. Still turned on and horny, I turned over on my back and spread my legs. I grabbed his dick and slowly stroked it to get the last bit of cum out.

I wrapped my legs around his neck and shoulders and pulled his sexy body down on top of me. I guided his still hard dick back into my pussy. He began to stroke it again then suddenly we saw someone walking in the distance. We instantly hopped up and ran as fast as we could up the sand dune, grabbed our clothes, and quickly put them on.

We gathered the rest of our things and made our way down the dune as we passed a group of teenagers who were out for a stroll. We both looked at each other and laughed as we thought about what they had on their minds and what they were going to do.

Later that night I asked Dylan, "What made you decide to go skinny dipping?"

Dylan responded by saying, "Tradition," and continued to say, "Every time I go to a beach, I like to get naked and take a run for the water." He explained, "It feels as if it cleanses my soul and I feel so free afterward."

I laughed and said, "I like traditions and would like to start some of my own."

CHAPTER 8
Marinating in the Sauce

After a few beautiful days at the beach, we took down the tent, packed up everything and headed home. We arrived at my house late that Sunday afternoon. I told Dylan, "I had a great time, and I do not want this to end."

He looked deep into my eyes and said, "Don't worry this is just the beginning of many new adventures for us."

We got out of the truck, Dylan grabbed my bags, and we headed to the door. He sat the bags down on the porch then he gave me a long kiss goodbye. I stared at him as he walked all the way to his truck. I continued to watch until the truck was out of my view. This is when I exhaled as I leaned against the porch column.

The kids were not scheduled to come back home until later, but I called to see how they were doing and just to let them know I was home. After talking to my parents, I took a shower, and curled up on my bed to take a nap. I woke up a few hours later from the ringing of the doorbell. At the door were the kids and my parents all wearing Hawaiian lays. The kids were excited, and both were trying to tell me about the Hawaiian festival my parents took them to.

My Dad even came in and began to Hula dance for me. We all laughed then Dad went to bring in all of the bags. The kids lent him a hand and proceeded to take their things upstairs.

Meanwhile, Mom sat me down on the couch.

She was smiling and asked, "How did your trip with *Prince Charming* go?"

I grabbed her hand and said, "Awesome."

She hugged me and said, "Fantastic."

I told her, "We had a magnificent time and I think he may be the one, but we had not discussed anything about making it an official relationship yet."

Mom told me, "When the time is right you will. Take this time to really enjoy each other's company and get to really know each other. If he is the one, it will eventually reveal itself in due time."

Dad returned from upstairs and asked Mom, "Are you ready?"

I gave both of them a hug and kiss, and then they left. I went upstairs to see the kids and to give them a big I miss you hug. Conner was in his room playing a dragon game on the Wii, and Morgan was in her room playing a fashion dress up game on her tablet. I headed back downstairs to grab my luggage then went to bed.

The next morning, I dropped the kids off at school and headed to *Wal-Mart* to pick up a few things. On the way home I realized that I forgot to get a bag of ice. I remembered seeing an old country store off the main road when Dad first gave us a tour around the town. It took me a while to find the place, but I finally did. It turns out that it was about a mile and a half from my house.

The store was timeworn and dilapidated on the outside. It had a sign that read *Stevens Country Store and Honey Bees founded in 1846*. The sign was old and looked like it was barely hanging on by a small thin wire.

I walked in, and the store had everything you could imagine stuffed into a very small place. A tall older man greeted me who was wearing a cowboy hat and coveralls.

He introduced himself, "Hello, I am Earl Stevens. It would be my pleasure to help you."

I was shocked that he was such a gentleman. I told him, "My name is Meadow Roberts and I need a bag of ice and some sugar."

Mr. Stevens said, "Well you came to the right place, now follow me to aisle three." He asked me, "Where are you from young lady?"

I told him, "*Pennsylvania*, I just moved here to be closer to my parents and I am living in my late Grandma's house down the road from here."

He had a stunned look on his face and asked, "Who is your Grandmother?"

I told him, "Lillie Thompson, but we called her Ma Lillie."

Mr. Stevens smiled, and his face lit up and was full of joy. He said, "I have not seen you since you were about six months old."

I was shocked and wondered, "What is going on? Who is this man?"

Mr. Stevens told me, "Come with me," as he took my hand and led me to the back of the store.

I was a little nervous, but he seemed harmless.

He led me to an open area with several tables and told me, "Have a seat."

He reached high up on a shelf and grabbed a dusty old book that turned out to be a photo album. Opening the album Mr. Stevens pulled out a picture of two young men in *Air Force* uniforms. I asked, "Who are they?"

He said, "This is me, and this fella right here was my best friend, who just so happens to be your Grandfather."

I smiled as he showed me several pictures of both of my Grandparents.

He repeatedly spoke of how, "They were real good people and I miss them dearly. Your Grandpa Eddie was an active, brave, and fearless man. He loved his country, and it was nothing more he wanted to do than fight for our freedom. I actually helped your Grandpa Eddie build the house that you live in now."

Mr. Stevens was so happy to hear that the house was not going to be torn down.

He went on to say, "Ma Lillie was the kindest, most loving, and most caring person I have ever met. She had the best-baked pies and cobblers in the land."

I mentioned to him that, "She left me her recipes, and I have made all of them at least once."

Mr. Stevens said, "Outstanding, I would like to try one of your pies and cobblers one day."

I told him, "I will make a special batch just for you."

Mr. Stevens said, "I would be grateful." He gathered the sugar and said, "I will get the ice on the way out." I began to head to the counter when Mr. Stevens stated, "It is on the house. Any family of the Thompson's are my family too. Around these parts, we take care of family."

I began to walk out when I saw several bottles of honey for sale. I asked Mr. Stevens, "Do you still have honey bees?"

He replied, "I have been a honey bee farmer for over 30 years." He asked, "Do you have any kids?"

I told him, "Yes, their names are Conner and Morgan."

He said, "You should bring them to the farm someday and I will give them a whole day of the total farm experience. I will even put them in the bee suits and let them help harvest the honey."

I told him, "That would be great and the kids would love it." Mr. Stevens grabbed a bag of ice, my bag of sugar, and a bottle of honey then put them in the car for me. He tipped his hat at me then I headed home to drop the stuff off before picking up the kids from school.

When I arrived at the school, there were more cars in the pickup line than usual. I saw my friend Patty and she reminded me that it was fundraiser pickup day. Conner and Morgan had raised a lot of money thanks to Mom and Dad. I parked the car and went to the office to pick up over 100 boxes of gourmet popcorn. I walked into the office and saw the office assistant Mrs. Henry. She was behind the counter making sure everyone received their correct orders.

When I finally got to the front of the line, Mrs. Henry said, "Oh yea, Roberts, we have your orders over here." She turned and pointed at a pallet stacked with boxes behind her.

I asked, "Are you sure?"

Mrs. Henry replied, "Yes mam, there are exactly187 different orders. Conner and Morgan sold more than any student in the entire school."

All I could say was, "Wow," and think of how happy I was to have taken the groceries to the house beforehand.

Mrs. Henry told me, "If you pull your car up to the front entrance, I will get the pallet jack and bring them out for you, then help you load them in your car. I did, and we loaded all of them into the trunk. Just as we finished, the end of day school bell rang and Conner and Morgan came running towards me and hopped into the car. I asked, "How was school?"

They both said, "It was good."

I told them, "I met an older gentleman named Mr. Stevens and he was a friend of your Great Grandparents. He has a country store and honey bee farm. You will be happy to know that he even invited you guys to spend a whole day with him on his farm."

They both were excited and asked, "When can we go?"

I laughed and told them, "Soon." Meanwhile, we needed to concentrate on getting all of these orders delivered. I will inform your Grandparents tomorrow so they can help you.

After dinner, Dylan called, and we talked about seeing each other this weekend. Our plan was for Dylan to come over and spend time at my house. We both enjoy cooking, so we decided to prepare a meal and spend some quality time at home. While the kids were going to be with my parents the whole weekend delivering orders of popcorn.

During the week the children attended several football and cheerleading practices. They seemed to like their teams and teammates, which helped make the whole transition easier. Friday afternoon my parents picked up the kids around 4:30 pm and Dylan arrived around 5:15 pm.

We both agreed that we were going to cook an Italian meal. We got in his truck and headed to the local *Publix* grocery store. I grabbed everything we needed to make Spaghetti while Dylan went to get what we needed to make a salad.

He was taking longer than anticipated, so I headed to the vegetable aisle to help him out. Dylan saw me coming his way and grabbed a cucumber. Holding the cucumber in his hand he began to let his drool of saliva drip down on the cucumber then proceeded to rub it into the cucumber as he stared at me with those intensely sexy eyes.

Forming his hand into the shape of a circle he slowly slid the cucumber in and out of his fingers in a very provocative way. I felt a little uneasy at first because we were in a public place and told him, "Stop," but of course, he did not.

I said, "What the heck," and began to play along. I bent over in front of him, and he slowly slid the cucumber up and between my legs. I began to let out a sexy moan as if we were really having sex. In the process of us playing around, we forgot where we were.

Suddenly, this elderly couple walking by told us, "Get a room!" We both looked at each other and laughed as we headed to the register to pay for our food. We left the store and laughed uncontrollably all the way home as we mocked the elderly couple.

Upon arrival back home, we gathered the groceries and placed them on the kitchen counter. I started to boil the water for the Spaghetti noodles and to prepare the ground beef and sauce. Dylan began to wash off the vegetables and prepare them for the salad. For whatever reason he suddenly stepped out of the kitchen. My guess was that he had to use the bathroom.

While he was gone, I began to slice the garlic bread and helped prepare the salad. The next thing I knew, something was sliding up my leg. When I turned around Dylan was holding a wooden spoon.

I started hitting him on his chest as he laughed at me. He placed the spoon on the counter, grabbed both of my ass cheeks, and began to squeeze one and caress the other.

He whispered in my ear and told me, "You have been a naughty girl!" He grabbed my ear lobe between his lips and then he told me, "It is time for your punishment!"

I politely said, "Ok, Mr. Sir!" and I assumed the position as I leaned over the counter. Dylan grabbed the wooden spoon and spanked my ass with it several times on each cheek.

He told me, "I wanted to see how long your ass cheeks would jiggle."

After a few more hard smacks, I continued my preparation of the salad, while he slowly pulled my skirt and panties to my ankles. There I stood butt naked from the waist down. I was making a salad, while he was tossing mine! My legs began to get very weak then they began to tremble.

I unbuttoned my blouse and pulled up my bra so my exposed breasts could hang and swing freely. I started rubbing my nipples but had to stop, so I could brace myself by holding onto the counter to prevent from falling. At this point, the water from the noodles were beginning to boil over. I did not want him to stop, but I did not want to ruin the noodles either. I pulled up my panties, straightened my skirt, and buttoned up my blouse.

We ended up draining the noodles and adding the ground beef to the sauce. I set the table and lit two candles. Dylan cut off the lights and turned on the radio that was playing *Sade's Soldier of Love* as we sat down and began to eat. Dylan grabbed his fork and began to feed me. I gazed into his eyes and was no longer hungry. I realized I was full off of the love I had for him. I got up from my chair and pushed the table away. I started kissing Dylan on his neck then performed a strip tease as I took off all of my clothes except my panties.

I turned around with my ass facing him as he sat in the chair. I spread my legs, bent over, and began to slowly slide my panties to my ankles. I looked back at him through the gap between my legs. He tried to grab my ass, but I smacked his hand away.

I turned around again and this time I pulled off his shorts, grabbed a cup of ice sitting on the table and sucked an ice cube into my mouth. I then proceeded to suck his dick until the ice cube melted completely. I turned around with my back facing him again and sat on his dick until it entirely disappeared inside of me. I slid up and down twice. With each stroke up and down I could feel and hear the gushing of my cum as it started to secrete down all over his dick and balls.

I got up and sat on his lap facing him. I began to tear the shirt off his chest and began to lick his pectoral muscles as I rode his dick. Dylan wrapped his arms underneath my legs and picked me up, as I wrapped my arms around his neck and held on. He carried me and placed me on the countertop.

I spread my legs as wide as I could get them as he swiped my clit with his tongue. It was so sensitive that it tickled, and I laughed as I closed my legs, for a few seconds then wrapped them around his neck and squeezed. I held him in my grips for a brief moment then let him go.

Dylan grabbed one of the cucumbers that we played with in the supermarket off the counter. He took the tip of it and began to rub it back and forth, on and around the top of my clit, while he licked the bottom part of my pussy, then placed it back on the counter.

Dylan took my feet and placed them on the countertop. Spreading them apart as he kissed my neck and licked down my chest. I grabbed my breasts and pushed them together as he began to lick and suck both of my nipples at the same time.

He proceeds to grab the cucumber again and teases me by rubbing it all around my clit again. I grabbed his hand, and guided the cucumber to my vagina. I then helped him slide it deep inside me. I moved his hand to the side and began to slide the cucumber in and out of my vagina as he watched in awe.

I could see that it turned him on, so I slid it even deeper inside me until it almost disappeared. I left it there as I stared into his eyes, then I gave him a passionate kiss.

Suddenly, Dylan reached down and slowly removed the cucumber, and then threw it across the room. He then replaced it by sliding his dick inside me. I could feel it pulsating as I laid my head back against the wall. With every stroke I could feel him in my stomach. Looking down at my stomach muscles I could see them rise up every time he went deep inside me. We fucked on the countertop for at least an hour. My pussy was so wet that my juices had accumulated all over the countertop and began to drip down the front of the drawers. Dylan's dick began to get warmer and he came all up inside me. I spread my pussy lips and let his cream pie drip down onto the floor.

Afterward, we cleaned up the kitchen, and took a shower together. Later we relaxed on the couch and watched television. I grabbed Dylan's hand and told him, "I want to talk about the letter you left on the bed. It was the most beautiful words put together for me that I had ever seen in my lifetime. I actually fell asleep with it lying on my chest that night."

Dylan told me, "It is how I really feel about you and I just had to capture those thoughts on paper."

I snuggled up close to him, and he held me tight.

Wheel of Fortune was on at the time, and the word had nine letters in it. It started with an "S," had 2 "C's," and ended with a "T."

The contestant asked for a letter, "L."

Pat Sajak said, "There is one "L."

We both simultaneously yelled out the word, "Succulent."

The contestant did the same.

Pat Sajak told the contestant, "That is correct," as *Vanna White* revealed the remaining letters.

Pat went on to explain the meaning of the word.

He said, "Wet, juicy, moist, tasty, fleshy, and rich in desirable qualities."

I told Dylan, "That is a good description of us." He smiled as he began to hold me tighter. We watched television the rest of the night until Dylan left to go home.

CHAPTER 9

Anatomy of a Motorcycle

The next few weeks were a little hectic, with football practices and games we had to attend. Dylan's team went undefeated during the season and were now in the playoffs. The first three playoff games went very well with them winning by an average of 21 points each game. There is yet one final game to be played, and it is the championship game against the perennial winner, *Florida Pop Warner Football* powerhouse the *Gainesville Gators.* The Gators have won the *Pop Warner* championship a record eight consecutive years in a row.

It is going to be a big challenge but not an impossible one to defeat them. Dylan and the team had one week to prepare. We talked and still saw each other occasionally, but I gave him his space as much as I could. I knew he and the team were preparing carefully for this important game.

During my free time, I thought about what Dylan and I discussed the last time he was at my house. I asked him, "What should I do with the money left to me by Ma Lillie?"

He told me, "You should start a business of some kind and that it should be something you have a passion for or something you love to do."

Days later while walking around downtown, I came across a building that was closed and had a for sale sign in the window. Looking at the sign the building use to be some type of bar or lounge before it closed. I saw a phone number, so I reached in my bag to find a pen.

Suddenly, the door opened, and a woman dressed in business suit attire came out. I asked her, "Are you the owner?"

She said, "Yes, I am." She introduced herself, "I am Regina Callaway," as she shook my hand.

Regina was an older lady with a warm and inviting smile. I told her, "My name is Meadow Roberts, and I am interested in seeing what your building has to offer."

Mrs. Callaway said, "Well sugar, come on in. I always have time for a potential client," as she unlocked the door.

My tour began with Mrs. Callaway explaining, "This place use to be a bar and lounge until my late husband died and I just no longer had the passion for keeping it open. It was something we did together, and I just could not do it without him there."

When we first walked in, there was a gathering area with bathrooms and a hallway that led to a large open area. This area contained a circular stage in the middle of the floor.

Mrs. Callaway commented, "It rotates 360 degrees."

On each side of the room were two bar areas. Walking toward the back of the building there was a door with a hallway that led to a small dressing room, a large storage area, and another door to a small kitchen. Everything was clean and in good condition. Overall, I was very impressed with the building and had already started envisioning what I could and wanted to do with this space.

After the tour, Mrs. Callaway gave me her business card and said, "If you are still interested, we can set up an appointment to discuss the financial details and go from there."

I said, "I would," and left with a good feeling about the building and Mrs. Callaway. I had several thoughts of what I wanted to do. The idea that stood out the most in my mind was a poetry lounge and learning center.

I thought about what I loved, and the answer was art and expression. I thought about what I had a passion for, and it was creativity and teaching. My idea was to have a place where people could come to express themselves, be creative, relax, share, and learn.

On a nightly basis, people could come to share themselves through poetry. On Friday nights, I would feature an up and coming band and the person with the best poem of the evening would win a monetary prize. I could sell Ma Lillie's pies and cobbler's along with beverages. I could also turn part of the storage area into a small classroom that would be used to teach art classes.

The next day I called my lawyer Tommy and told him, "I have found some property I would like to purchase," and told him about my vision I had for it.

He was happy to hear from me and advised me to, "Call Mrs. Callaway and set up a meeting with her to discuss what it would take to get a deal done, then hire a building inspector to check out the building before signing or agreeing to anything. If everything checks out, I will draw up a proposal offer to be given to Mrs. Callaway, and if she accepted the offer, the property will be yours."

I immediately called Mrs. Callaway after getting off the phone with Tommy and set up a meeting for the next morning at 9:00 am. The kids would be in school, and that would give me plenty of time to discuss business.

I was so excited the next morning and was rushing to get the kids to school. After dropping them off, I was on my way to Mrs. Callaway's office. She was located about eight miles outside of *Homestead* in *Florida City*. It turned out to be the corporate headquarters of the *Callaway Corporation*. I was impressed as I pulled up to a building consisting of all glass with five floors and a big fountain in the front courtyard.

I went inside and headed to the elevator. When the door opened at the fifth floor there was a receptionist waiting for me.

She told me, "Have a seat and Mrs. Callaway will be with you shortly." The young lady asked, "Would you like coffee or anything else to drink?"

I told her, "No thanks." I glanced around the room and could see photos of all the properties Mrs. Callaway owned and they looked very impressive.

A few minutes later, Mrs. Callaway came and greeted me with a, "Hey sugar!" and a big hug. She told me, "Come in my office so we can talk." Her personality and loving spirit made me feel at home and helped me relax. Mrs. Callaway then said, "I see you are very interested in the property on South street?"

I responded, "Yes, I am."

Mrs. Callaway said, "Before we go any further, I need to know what you plan to do with the property?"

I told her, "I want to turn it into a poetry lounge where people could come and enjoy other people being free and creative while expressing themselves through poetry and music. I am going to name it *Poetry and Pie Lounge & Learning Center*. The pie part comes from my Grandma's recipes for pies and cobblers. Without my Grandma's help, none of this would be possible, so I plan to sell them at the lounge. I also plan to make part of the storage area into a classroom where I will teach art classes."

Mrs. Callaway said, "Well you seem to have excellent ideas. I am very impressed with how you intertwined the sentimental value of your Grandma into your vision," she went on to say, "You know I like you and your spirit, and because I do, I will sell you the property for only $42,000. It is worth way more than that, and I have had offers for about ten times that amount, but to me it is about keeping my late husband's dream alive. He put his heart and soul into that place, and I wanted to ensure that the person I sold it to would take care of it and not destroy it."

I was shocked and did not know what to say but, "Thank you!" I told her, "Give me a chance to talk to my lawyer and pending a building inspection we had a deal."

Mrs. Callaway said, "I am good with that just let me know when you get an inspector so I can meet you there."

We shook hands, and I gave her a hug. I left and was on cloud nine the whole way home.

The next day was Saturday and the day of the big championship game. The kids were excited and nervous at the same time. Dylan was calm, but I know deep down inside he had some butterflies but was not going to let them show. We all rode to the game together. When we arrived, I pulled Conner to the side and gave him an encouraging pep talk. I told him, "Give your all and do the best you can, and no matter what the outcome, you will always be a winner!"

Conner said, "I know Mom," with a big smile and gave me a hug before he ran to join his teammates.

I grabbed Dylan's hand and told him, "You will always be my champion," and told him, "Give them hell!" He laughed and then gave me a kiss before he too ran to join his team.

I went up into the stands and grabbed me a seat as I watched Morgan and her cheer squad warming up. I screamed her name and blew her a big kiss then formed both of my hands in the shape of a heart. She smiled and then blew me a kiss back. She also formed her hands in a heart symbol back to me. Mom and Dad joined me a few minutes later, and they were all decked out in *Florida City Razorback* gear.

Finally, it was kick off time. The game started off slow and seemed as if it was going to be a long defensive battle. Neither team was able to move the ball down the field. At the end of the first quarter, the score was 0-0. The second quarter was no different with each team turning the ball over with a fumble and an interception but again the quarter ended with two goose eggs 0-0.

The third quarter started off with the *Gainesville Gators* kickoff returner running the kickoff back for a touchdown. The Gator fans were hyped and excited. I was a little nervous but not discouraged. After *Gainesville* scored Dylan huddled the whole team around him and gave them an uplifting pep talk.

The huddle broke, and the players began to do some kind of dance and chant that I had never seen them do, but whatever it was it got them refocused and ready to play again. They ran back on the field with a different type of swagger and confidence. It was evident from the first snap when they ran a play action fake, and the quarterback threw a bomb down the field for 20 yards to Conner who avoids two tackles and takes it all the way to the end zone.

I jumped up and down and did the same little dance myself. I was so happy and just kept repeating, "That's my boy!" Now the momentum was on our Razorback side. The quarter ended with the score tied 7-7.

Here we were with only one quarter left and once again we went back and forth with neither team being able to move the ball down the field. The time was winding down and only three minutes remained on the clock. *Gainesville* had the ball on their 10-yard line and began to put together a drive that looked like they were the *New England Patriots*. They drove the ball all the way down to our 20-yard line, and it was third and three. Our defense was tired and seemed to be back on their heels. If we hold them, we will have one last chance to score.

Gainesville hiked the ball, and it was handed off to the tailback for a draw play. He took the handoff and started towards the right side of the field when one of our linebackers met him head on picked him up and drove him to the ground. The ball popped out of his hands just as the linebacker hit him. There was a mad scramble for the ball but it was recovered by a *Gainesville* player for about a 20-yard loss. Everyone came over and gave him a high five and began to do that special dance once again.

Gainesville punted and we returned the ball to our 20-yard line. The offense ran onto the field with only 2 minutes 30 seconds remaining in our season or we were going into overtime. The first play from scrimmage was a draw play, and our running back ran for 7 yards on the right side. The next play Dylan called a passing play.

The quarterback threw a pass to a receiver running a post route. It was for a 1st down and a gain of 20 yards. We were now on our 47-yard line, with 1 minute 46 seconds left on the clock. There were just 53 yards left for us to overcome before we would be crowned champions.

The quarterback lined up in a shotgun formation and hiked the ball. The *Gainesville* defense sent the house rushing after him. He barely escaped but managed to scramble and ended up completing another pass for 30 yards, to a wide receiver before they tackled him out of bounds. The clock stopped with just 56 seconds left in the game. Now we were on the *Gainesville* 23-yard line. The next three plays we just could not move the ball down the field at all. We had a ball knocked down, a dropped pass, and a run that only got back to the line of scrimmage.

At this time the clock had 9 seconds left on it. Dylan called a timeout and sent in the field goal unit, but this time, Conner was out there with them as the holder. He was never part of the field goal unit, so I was shocked and wondered what was going on.

The center hiked the ball, Conner grabbed it and instead of placing it down for the kicker he stands up and tosses it back to the kicker. Conner then ran a slant towards the left corner of the end zone. The kicker under pressure threw a pass to Conner who was wide open in the end zone. It seemed like the pass took an eternity to get to him as it just seemed to float and hang in the air. Conner reached out to catch the ball but juggled it before pulling it in while tiptoeing to get his two feet down before his momentum carried him out of the end zone, as the time ran out on the clock.

All of the *Florida City Razorback* fans jumped up and ran onto the field. Dylan was the first person to get to Conner, he picked him up and put him on his shoulders as the team, and fans chanted, "Razorbacks!", "Razorbacks!"

I ran onto the field uncontrollably to join them. Conner somehow saw me and Dylan let him down. I placed my hands on his cheeks and looked into his eyes and told him, "I am so proud of you," as tears of joy started to flow down my cheeks.

He hugged me tight and told me, "Thanks Mom."

I went to Dylan and gave him a big kiss and told him, "You are a genius to call such a deceptive but gutsy play."

Dylan told me, "We ran that play every practice, but never used it in a game because I was keeping it for the right situation." He went on to say, "I had faith in the kicker being able to make the pass but more importantly, I had faith in Conner being able to catch it. Plus, I did not want to risk missing the field goal or having it blocked. My main concern was that I did not want to go into overtime because the team was physically exhausted."

After being presented with the championship trophies and the celebration on the field slowly coming to an end, we decided to continue it and take the team to *Pizza Inn*. My Mom and Dad were like our team mascots. They kept the celebration fun and exciting. Especially, when they learned the dance the kids did on the field and made up their own version of it. We all laughed for hours at them.

The next day while washing a few clothes I heard a roaring sound. When I looked out of the window, I saw a man on a motorcycle coming up the pathway. The engine roared even more the closer he got to the house. I looked closer and realized it was Dylan. I ran outside to greet him.

He took off his helmet and said, "After several long and stressful weeks, I figured we would go for a long relaxing victory ride on my motorcycle."

I told him, "You are in luck because my parents are on the way and should be here in about 5 minutes. They are coming to visit, and Dad is going to help the kids start a garden."

They arrived a few moments later and greeted Dylan with a hug and congratulated him again. I told them, "We were thinking about taking a ride."

My Mom immediately said, "Go ahead, your Dad will help the kids with the garden, and I will finish doing the laundry I see you have already started."

I went inside and put on a short skirt and placed my hair into a ponytail and came back downstairs. I grabbed the helmet and placed it on my head, got on the bike, and wrapped my arms around Dylan's waist. He cranked the bike, and there was a roar from the engine that vibrated throughout my whole body.

Dylan took off, and I blew a kiss to the kids as we departed. We rode for about 3 miles, and I began to see the beautiful landscape change. It started off with palm trees and brush, but after about 45 minutes there were just open fields and farmland.

I could see a rather large tree in the distance, and it seemed that Dylan was heading that way. We eventually pulled up to the large tree that had long thin branches that draped down towards the ground. It turned out to be a *Weeping Willow* tree.

I took off my helmet and hopped off the back of the bike. I jumped back on the front of the bike facing Dylan while the engine was still running. I wanted to make love to his eyes, so I started stripping off my shirt and bra, exposing my full breasts to him. I grabbed both of them in my hands and began to squeeze them together. I licked one of my nipples and fondled the other.

Dylan turned the bike off and started to suck on the nipple that I was not licking. He then began to lick my body from my belly button until he reached my exposed nipples again. At this point they were erect and extra sensitive because they were yearning for his tongue and lips to bless them again.

He grabbed my nipples and began to caress them slowly and gently. Dylan then began to twist them slowly until I moaned out loud. I placed one of my nipples on his lips, and he started sucking it until I came all over my hand that was inside my panties.

I could not take it anymore, so I flipped over on my stomach and straddled the gas tank with my ass up facing him. The only thing I had on was a skirt and my panties. He sat on the bike behind me and kissed the back of my neck. I leaned forward then he grabbed my panties and pulled them to the side as he fondled my pussy lips from the back. I told him, "Give it to me!" He grabbed my panties and began to rip them off of me. A few seconds later I felt his long erect dick slowly penetrating my insides. I arched my back and laid my head on the handlebars as he fucked my exposed wet pussy. He paused for a brief second to crank the bike and it felt like a human vibrator as his stiff dick began to vibrate inside me.

My pussy was being stroked while my clit was vibrating from the engine through the gas tank. He grabbed my ponytail wrapped it around his hand and began to pull my hair every time he stroked. It was so good that it made my eyes water. I flipped over on my back and he began to fuck me while I was sucking my own nipples again. He grabbed both of my ankles and pushed them towards the handlebars, spreading my legs as wide as I and he could get them, giving him even more pussy access.

Every stroke felt as if it took my breath. I could not help it, but I came all over his dick and the gas tank. Dylan pulled out and came all over my chest. It felt like I was having a warm afternoon rain shower all over me.

We cleaned up and sat underneath the tree hugged up while watching the sunset. About an hour later we decided to head back to *Homestead*. We were both a little thirsty, so, I told Dylan, "I know of a store on the way back owned by a man named Mr. Stevens who is a friend of the family." We stopped by to get something to drink and Mr. Stevens was in the back sitting at one of the tables talking with his friends and playing checkers.

He was happy to see me again, and I was glad to see him. I introduced Dylan to him, and they shook hands.

Mr. Stevens said, "Much obliged young man." He then asked, "What can I do for you?"

I told him, "We just stopped by to say hello and to get something to drink."

Mr. Stevens asked, "Do you want an Icee, juice, or soda?"

I told him, "A *Cheerwine* soda for me."

Dylan said, "A *Mountain Dew.*"

Mr. Stevens reached into the cooler and grabbed a hard bottle long neck *Cheerwine* and *Mountain Dew.*

He popped off the tops and asked, "Would you like anything else?"

We both told him, "We are good."

Mr. Stevens and I stood against the counter and talked for several minutes. Dylan began to walk around the store looking up at the beams in the ceiling.

He told Mr. Stevens, "The building was very historic and that it had beautiful Architecture, but the roof had started to leak possibly causing damage to some of the structural beams."

Mr. Stevens said, "I have noticed the roof had begun leaking but just never got around to fixing it. I have a hard time climbing up ladders now."

Dylan and I glanced at each other and smiled.

Dylan told Mr. Stevens, "I am a general contractor, and I do renovations. I can fix it for you and check out the structural beams if you like."

Mr. Stevens said, "That would be great. I also have a few other building projects for you if you are interested."

Dylan said, "Sure, we will set up a time for me to come back and check everything out."

Dylan and Mr. Stevens shook hands as we walked back to the bike. We left and got back home about 15 minutes later. I walked into the house and smelled something cooking on the stove. We walked into the kitchen, and the table was full of food and Mom, Dad, and the kids were all sitting at the table. There were two other plates with food already on them.

Dad said "Join us, good people," and we sat down.

I told Mom, "You did not have to do this."

She said, "Baby, I wanted to do it."

On the plates were *Cornish Hens* with stuffing, corn on the cobb, and greens. We had a very entertaining dinner. Dad, as always provided the entertainment. He told jokes and made up exaggerated stories. I don't know how we finished our meal because we did more laughing than we did eating.

The next day the kids and I got up early and went for a walk through the trails in the woods behind our pond. The trails seemed to have come from people riding dirt bikes and ATV's.

We also saw all kinds of animal life from Hummingbirds, flying insects, and especially bees. The bees reminded me of Mr. Stevens and his Honeybee Farm. When we got back from our walk, we hopped in the car and went to the grocery store.

On our return from the store, I began to make Ma Lillie's pies and cobblers for Mr. Stevens, just as I promised him I would. When I finished, I placed them on a table outside on the porch so they could cool.

While waiting, I decided I was going to make Mr. Stevens a new sign for his store. I remembered how worn out the current one was and just felt it would be a nice thing to do and just something I needed to do. I wanted the sign to incorporate his honeybee farm but also accent the country store feel of his store as well. It took a few hours, but I was very satisfied with the results. I hoped he would be too.

CHAPTER 10

Property of Mine

The next day I received a call from Tommy. He had reviewed the contract for the purchase of Mrs. Callaway's property.

He told me, "Everything looked good."

Earlier in the week we had a building inspector come and inspect the structure. It not only passed inspection but the inspector deemed it to be in excellent condition. I was excited because this was step one of my vision coming true. I could not wait to tell Dylan, but I wanted to do it in a special way.

After finishing Mr. Steven's sign for his store last night, I called him and made plans to bring the kids over for their all-day farm experience. The free time would allow me to go to the lounge and finish setting up and finalizing a few last details for the grand opening in a few weeks.

I gathered the pies I made for Mr. Stevens and placed them securely in the car while I waited for the kids to finish getting ready. I wrapped up the sign I made for him and put a bow on it. The kids hopped in the car, and we were on our way.

We pulled into the driveway of Steven's Farm and the kids got extra excited. They could see farm animals in a fence and other animals roaming free. I parked in front of the farmhouse and the kids hopped out and immediately started chasing after the chickens.

Mr. Stevens came to the door and laughed, as he watched them running from one end of the yard to the other. I yelled for the kids and told them, "Stop," but they just ignored me and kept on chasing the chickens.

Mr. Stevens said, "It's ok, let them have fun. I will take good care of them. You go and do what you need to do."

I told him, "Ok," but before I left, I surprised him with the pies and cobblers I had made.

He was ecstatic and repeatedly, said, "Um, um, um, I can't wait to try these out. Thank you so much!"

I helped him take all of them inside. When we came back outside, I called for the kids to come so I could say goodbye. I told them, "I will be back later tonight."

I got in my car and heard Mr. Stevens ask the kids, "Are you ready to have fun?"

The reply was a loud, "Yes!"

I laughed and drove away at peace because I knew they were in good hands. When I got back on the main road, I realized I forgot to give him his sign. I was going to turn around but decided just to give it to him at a later date.

I was on my way to my new property to meet Mrs. Callaway. I pulled up in front of the building and saw Tommy and Mrs. Callaway conversing with each other outside. I got out of the car, and she immediately handed the keys to me. I hesitated and paused for a minute only because I saw the doors had a big red bow and ribbon on them.

Tommy and Mrs. Callaway both told me, "Go ahead," as he handed me some scissors.

I was smiling from ear to ear and cut the ribbon as fast as I could. When I opened the door, what I saw was immaculate. Everything was shining like new, plus there were several big boxes stacked in the corner. I asked, "What's in the boxes?"

Mrs. Callaway said, "When you told me your vision, I was so touched that I wanted to do something special for you. I bought all new kitchen equipment, lighting, sound equipment, art tables and art supplies for you. I also had them equip the bar area with fountain drink capability. Plus, I had a cleaning company come and clean the whole building from top to bottom inside and out."

I was so full of joy that I began to cry. I grabbed her and hugged her like she was my Mother. I told her, "Thank you!" over and over again.

Mrs. Callaway said, "Wait, there is more. I also set aside a $100,000 grant for your art classes and will be making another $100,000 donation that can be used for the winners of the poetry contests."

I was speechless at first but then said, "I cannot accept this. It would be like I was getting the property for free."

Mrs. Callaway stopped me, and said, "Sugar, I believe in you and your vision, and I have a deep love for the arts. Also, I have not been so happy and inspired since my late husband died. You made me want to continue to live just like he would have wanted me to, instead of just mourning him the rest of my life. You sparked a rejuvenation in me that had not existed for years. This is my thanks to you."

She formed her hands into a heart as she got into her car and drove away.

Tommy turned towards me and said, "Wow!"

I told him, "She must be my guardian angel."

I stayed at *Poetry and Pie* for several hours moving the boxes to the storage room. When I left it was about 9:00 pm and I headed to *Steven's Farm* to pick up the kids. The weather had begun to change as dark clouds began to roll in and it started to rain. I picked up the kids then we headed home. They started to tell me all about how they milked cows, fed chickens, collected eggs but their favorite thing they did was working with the honeybees.

I asked them, "What did you do with the bees?"

They replied, "We put on these funny white suits that covered everything except our face. We then took this hat with a mask on the front and placed it over our heads. It felt like we were Astronauts."

Conner said, "Mr. Stevens then took us to the bee hives, and we began to harvest the honey."

They both were excited and asked, "When can we go back?"

I told them, "I am glad you had a good time, and I will talk it over with Mr. Stevens to see."

We decided to watch a movie when we got home so I popped some popcorn. The rain began to come down even harder than before and developed into a violent thunderstorm. There was thunder that rumbled and shook the house and lightning that lit up the sky. Suddenly, there was a loud banging on the door. I looked through the peephole, and Dylan was standing on the porch soaking wet from head to toe.

I opened the door and immediately asked, "What is wrong? Are you ok?" He just began to sob as he dropped to his knees. I hollered for Morgan and told her, "Bring me a towel!" I grabbed the towel and began to dry him off. I held him in my arms on the floor of the porch and asked him again, "What's wrong?" Dylan continued to cry and did not respond to any of my questions, so I just held him and rocked back and forth as I tried to keep his body warm.

A few minutes went by and Dylan began to finally calm down. I helped him inside and he eventually told us what was wrong with him.

He said, "My mother passed away this morning in her sleep."

He then began to sob and cry all over again. This time, Conner came over, and we all shared a group hug. Dylan was in no condition to drive back home, so I got him some dry clothes he had left over previously. He laid on the couch and I told him, "I will go pick up Casey from her caretaker's house."

When we arrived at the caretaker's house, Casey looked surprised then asked, "Where is my Dad?"

I felt that Dylan should be the one to tell her, but he was in no condition to do so. I grabbed Casey by her hands, looked directly into her eyes, and told her, "Your Father is at my house mourning the death of your Grandmother."

Casey said, "No, not Grandma Ana!" and then she started to cry.

I pulled her close to me and held her as tight as I could. I told her, "They found your Grandma early this morning unresponsive in her bed."

Casey told me, "I spoke to her for a few minutes yesterday and she seemed fine."

I rubbed her hair as she laid her head on my shoulder and told her, "Sometimes when it is your time to go, God does not give a warning. Your Grandma's mission of life was complete, so God took her to rest in Heaven." We slowly walked to the car, and I drove us home.

When we got home and walked into the living room, Dylan was knocked out sleep on the couch. I got a blanket and placed it over him. The kids and I headed upstairs. Conner went to his room. Morgan and Casey were in my bed as I held Casey in my arms for several hours until she cried herself to sleep. I ended up sleeping in the reclining chair beside the bed.

The next morning, I got up, and the girls and Conner were still asleep. I went downstairs to check on Dylan, and he was still sleep too. I did not want to wake him, so I headed to the kitchen and began to fix some breakfast. I guess the aroma of bacon and eggs must have caused him to wake up.

He came into the kitchen and said, "I am starving!"

I looked into his eyes and began to straighten his hair out of his face. He leaned his forehead onto mine and gave me a kiss.

He then told me, "Thank you for picking up Casey and for everything you have done for us."

Dylan then headed upstairs to take a shower. Conner and Morgan came down moments later just as I had just finished cooking. Casey was still upstairs sleep. I told the kids, "Go wash your face and hands in the powder room." When they got back, I had them set the table. We waited for a while for Dylan to come down but he never did.

I started to get concerned and told the kids, "I am going to go check on Dylan." The further I got up the stairs the more nervous I became. I saw the door to the hall bath was open, and the light was off. I headed to my room and slowly opened the door. I heard some sniffling and crying and saw Dylan hugging and consoling Casey, as I got closer, I saw they both were crying.

I was sad for them, and my heart went out to both of them for their loss. I joined them on the edge of the bed, and we cried together for about ten minutes until we heard Conner and Morgan's voices coming upstairs calling my name. We all dried our eyes as quickly as we could because none of us wanted them to see us crying, nor did we want to upset them.

They came in asking, "What is going on?" and said, "Mom, we are hungry!"

I said, "Ok, let's go eat." We all headed downstairs, and they sat around the table as I placed the food in the middle. We passed everything around, blessed the food, and began to eat. Afterward, I washed the dishes while Dylan called and made funeral and travel arrangements. I sat beside him on the couch when I was finished and told him, "I will go with you and Casey to the funeral."

Dylan said, "I appreciate the gesture, but you do not have to go with us."

I insisted and told him, "I want to go."

Dylan said, "Ok" and seemed relieved. He stated that, "Casey and I are going to leave tomorrow."

I told him, "I will join you the day before the funeral, allowing myself time to get the kids situated."

I dropped Casey and Dylan off at the airport the next day and told them, "I will see you in a few days." My parents came later and picked up the kids, but I still had not told them about my purchase of the lounge. My plan was to inform them when I got back from *Pennsylvania*.

Leaving my house, I headed downtown to the lounge. I had a sound and lighting guy, who was going to meet me there, to put the final touches on my stage. When I finally left the lounge that night, everything was complete. The stage, the lighting, the lounge area, and even the classrooms were all set up.

I got home and finished packing for my trip. A couple of days later I took an *Uber* to the airport and found out my flight had been delayed for one hour. When I finally was able to board the plane, I was a little nervous because I was going back to *Pennsylvania*.

The place where my ex-husband lives but also where my ex-best-friend Sara lives. I knew I was not going to see them, but I still had some reservations about going back. I closed my eyes and just eventually went to sleep.

When I woke, we were about to land. I got off the plane, waited for my bags, then went to rent a car. Dylan had insisted on picking me up, but I told him no. I just wanted him to spend as much time with his family as he could. I was coming to be supportive not to be a distraction.

After about a 50-minute drive from *Williamsport Regional Airport*, I arrived in the town of *Mansfield, Pennsylvania*. I followed Dylan's directions and finally pulled up to his Mom's house. There were several cars in the driveway, and the door had a big floral wreath on it. I got out and walked to the door. It opened, and there stood Dylan and Casey. Casey pushed Dylan out of the way just so she could give me a hug.

They invited me inside and introduced me to all of their family which included lots of Aunts, Uncles, Nieces, and Nephews. They all greeted me with a group hug then we all sat down in the family room. Different family members began to reminisce and tell stories about Mrs. Ana. It was very nice to hear all of the good things about someone who had lost their life. Then put the stories together creating your own separate vision of who that person was.

Afterward, everyone took their place at the dinner table and we did more laughing than we did eating. I was amazed at the family's closeness and how they made me feel right at home, even in this terrible time of grief.

Later that night as everyone was winding down and heading to bed, Dylan and I went outside and sat on the porch swing. He wrapped his arms around me and held me tight while we watched the fireflies light up the sky late into the night.

The mood was entirely different the next morning. Everyone was in a somber mood, as family members realized this would be the last time, they would see Mrs. Ana. No one was talking, but there was a lot of crying. It was truly a sad time, and I could see how much Mrs. Ana was truly loved.

I held Dylan's hand, and I constantly rubbed his back in a soft calming way. The limos pulled up to the house, and all of the family was taken to *Whispering Rivers Baptist Church* where Mrs. Ana was a member for over 40 years. When we arrived at the church you could see an outpouring of people lined up down the block waiting to pay their last respects to her. We walked in, and everyone immediately began to cry all over again as Ms. Ana's body laid in the casket in front of them.

The service began, and the church choir sang a beautiful song followed by words of encouragement from friends and family members. It was now time for the eulogy.

Dylan told me, "I will be back."

I thought he was going to the bathroom, but he headed towards the podium. I had no idea he was going to do the eulogy. Dylan spoke confidently and elegantly of his Mother and everyone in the church seemed to be in agreement with everything he was saying.

Summing it all up by stating, "Mom's whole life was a sacrifice for all of us." He ended the eulogy by saying, "My Mom may not have been the most popular person nor did she have a lot of close friends, but she was still a very important person, who had a positive impact on everyone she encountered. To have been embraced with her presence was truly a blessing. Now she has taken her rightful place and her soul is resting in heaven." He pointed toward the rafters of the church and said, "Love you Mom!"

I met Dylan halfway down the aisle. His face was filled with tears as I helped him back to the pew. He laid his head on my shoulder and I told him, "I am so proud of you!"

After the funeral and before proceeding to the gravesite a tall skinny woman in all black with a large black hat, sunglasses, and a black veil approached Dylan and myself as we waited outside to get back into the limo.

This woman walked up to us and tried to give Dylan a hug, but Dylan brushed her off and asked, "What are you doing here?"

The lady responded by lifting up her veil and took off her sunglasses then said, "Well, hello to you to my husband! I heard about my Mother-In-Law, and I came to pay my respects."

She had a cunning smile on her face as she said it.

Dylan grabbed my hand and said, "Let's go."

I then realized who this woman was.

It was Hillary, the ex-wife. She grabbed Dylan by the shoulder and told him, "You did not introduce me to your new bimbo!"

Dylan began to turn around and address her, but I stopped him. Instead, I got in her face and said, "You must be the bitch named Hillary? Well, my name is Meadow, and you need to show some respect to all of these grieving people." I moved closer to her face and whispered in a soft calm manner in her ear, "Before I mop the cement with your skinny ass!"

I then rubbed down the left side of her face with my index finger. Daring her to make one wrong move or to make another slick comment out of her mouth.

She shouted out, "Well I never!" She then ran off to her car.

I was glad Casey was in the limo and did not see our encounter. I would never want to disrespect her Mother in front of her.

Two days later Dylan was making arrangements for Mrs. Ana's belongings and everyone seemed to be getting back to normal as much as they could. I told Dylan, "I have decided to go back to *Florida* in the morning."

Dylan said, "Ok, I understand," he continued to say, "Thank you for being patient and understanding. Casey and I are going to stay another week, just to tie up some loose ends and to get everything taken care of with Mom's estate."

The next morning, I told them, "Goodbye," hopped in my rental car, and headed to the airport. Several hours later I arrived back in *Florida*. My parents and the kids were waiting for me as I entered the terminal door. Dad grabbed my bags, and we hopped in the car.

They all asked, "How are Dylan and Casey?"

I told them, "They took Mrs. Ana's passing really hard but they are doing ok."

I told Dad, "Please head towards downtown *Homestead*. I want to stop at this new place I saw." When we got downtown, I directed Dad to my lounge, and I had him park in front of the door. I told everyone, "Let's get out," and then I began to explain, "This is my new property. I named it *Poetry and Pie Lounge & Learning Center*. The lounge will be a place of expression of poetry and music. The pie part will be a tribute and a passing of the torch of the family recipes from Ma Lillie. The learning center will be where art and creativity will come together and be nurtured endlessly on a daily basis. Now come inside so I can show you around."

I opened the door, and they all ran inside. The first impression I got from them was an overwhelming, "Wow." I gave them a tour of the place, and they were all impressed and happy for me.

Especially, my parents, who told me, "We are so proud of you!"

I told them, "I am set to have my grand opening when Dylan gets back from *Pennsylvania*." I went on to say, "I have not told Dylan about my lounge and I have a special surprise planned for him that night."

They stated, "We cannot wait."

CHAPTER 11
Mural of Time

One week after my return to Florida, I received a call from Dylan.

He said, "Casey and I will be returning home tomorrow morning."

I said, "Great, I will be there to pick you up when you arrive." The next day I waited at the airport as the plane landed, and I watched it taxi up to the terminal. I was so excited as the passengers began to come through the door.

Finally, there he was again, the man of my dreams. I ran to him and jumped into his arms. He lifted me up and began to spin me around, then he let me down.

Casey ran to me and gave me a big hug too. I told her, "I missed you and I am so glad you are back." Dylan's whole demeanor was totally different from the day I left him in *Pennsylvania*. It was as if he was back to his old self.

On the way home, Dylan told me, "I am in a better place now as far as being able to deal with my Mom's death. It will always be a painful piece missing in my heart but each day seems to get a little better."

I said, "I know baby," as I rubbed his face.

Pulling up to Dylan's house I told him, "I will see you tomorrow." I just wanted to give him time to unpack his stuff and get some much-needed rest.

The next morning the kids and I spent a lot of time scrambling to put up and hand out flyers I had made for the grand opening of *Poetry & Pie* which was tonight at 8 pm.

Before Dylan came back, I had made arrangements with Casey's caretaker Amanda. Amanda had agreed to take all three kids to see the latest *Twilight* movie and then they were to spend the night at her place.

We dropped the twins off and Casey was already there. I left and headed to the lounge to make sure my employees, made up of a wait staff, two bartenders, kitchen staff, and a lounge manager had everything they needed. On my way home I called Dylan and told him, "I will pick you up at 7:30pm." It was now 6:00 pm.

Dylan said, "I will be ready and waiting." I took a shower when I got home, but all I could think of was how would he react to my special surprise.

My dress was already laid out on the bed. I put it on and sat in front of the mirror and began to comb my hair. I walked out of the house at 7:00pm. I pulled up to Dylan's house around 7:30pm and we made our way to the lounge.

Dylan tried to be slick and ask, "What do you have planned for me?"

I told him, "Be patient, and you will see." Dylan's facial expression became more puzzled the closer we got to downtown.

We finally pulled into the *Poetry & Pie* parking lot and I was in awe because to my surprise the parking lot was filled with cars.

Dylan asked, "What is this?"

I told him, "Remember when I asked what you think I should do with the money from Ma Lillie?"

He nodded and said, "Yes."

I told him, "I took your advice and invested in a business of things that I am passionate about, which are being creative and free expression."

We went inside, and I told the manager, "Take Dylan to the VIP section where my parents will be waiting." I headed back to my private dressing room to freshen up before I went on stage to introduce myself to the audience. My lounge manager came and got me when it was time.

The place was standing room only as I walked onstage. I said, "Hello everyone my name is Meadow Roberts. I am the owner and welcome to *Poetry & Pie Lounge and Learning Center*. Tonight, my dreams and wishes have definitely come true. I would like to thank each and every one of you for being here to share this experience with me. A special thanks to my parents, my two beautiful twins, Mrs. Callaway, and my wonderful boyfriend Dylan. Thank all of you for being so supportive of me." The audience applauded then all of a sudden, my Dad stood up and began to take a bow.

We all laughed and then I told everyone, "Drink, eat, snap your fingers, and enjoy the show." I introduced the first act, which was an up and coming band named *Controversy*.

I was ushered off the stage and took my seat beside Dylan.

He commented, "This place is beautiful, and I love it."

I told him, "Thanks babe," as I rubbed his hand.

The next several acts were poets, and the crowd was really into each one of them. They cheered and snapped their fingers for every performer while eating and drinking. We offered small finger foods, which included chicken strips, wings, fries, and of course Ma Lillie's mini pies and cobblers.

Now it was time for me to announce the winner of the poetry contest. I went on stage and said, "The first winner of poetry night is, *Word Magic!*" He received a plaque and a prize of $300.

Afterward, I told everyone, "Before you leave, I have a surprise." Everyone standing up began to sit back down. "It is a special poem that I want to dedicate to a special friend. It is called, *"What Is A Soulmate by Emily Matthews."* I turned to Dylan, and said, "Baby, I dedicate this poem to you!" The audience stood up and began to applaud Dylan. Once they settled down, I began to read the poem.

What Is A Soul Mate

If you have found a smile
that is the sweetest one you've known,

If you have heard, within a voice,
the echoes of your own,

If you have felt a touch
that stirs the longings of your heart,

And still can feel that closeness
in the moments you're apart,

If you have been filled with wonder
at the way two lives can blend

To weave a perfect pattern
that is seamless, end to end,

If you believe some things
are simply meant to be,

Then you have found your soul mate,
your heart's only destiny.

Emily Matthews

When I finished, Dylan met me on stage, and I melted in his arms all over again.

He whispered in my ear; "I have a surprise for you too."

I looked at him and said, "Ok."

He said, "I want you to come back to my place."

While all of this was going on the crowd was on their feet giving us a standing ovation and chanting, "Kiss, kiss, kiss!"

We kissed and then I thanked them for coming and took a bow. Dylan and I walked off the stage together holding hands.

On the way to my car we passed my parents who told me, "We loved the show, and your poem was beautiful!"

I told them, "Thank you, and I will see you tomorrow."

Dylan opened the passenger door to my car, and I got in. I was a little tired, so I took a quick nap on the way to his house. When we arrived, Dylan pulled out a blindfold and put it over my eyes. He then picks me up and carries me up the steps and into the house. Once inside he took me to a room and laid me down on a bed. He told me he would be right back as he walked out of the room. I laid on the bed with the blindfold still on. My mind was racing, and I was excited about what was going to happen next.

Dylan came back into the room and told me, "Take off the blindfold."

I did and standing directly in front of me still in the dark was Dylan totally naked with a blue neon glow in the dark cock ring around his dick.

I laughed and said, "Wow!"

I was about to suck it, but Dylan opened his hands and said, "Pick one."

There were two small bottles one in each of his hands. I grabbed one and looked at it. It was a bottle of blue glow in the dark body paint. I looked at the other one, and it was yellow glow in the dark body paint.

I told him, "Lay down on your back," as I took the head of his dick into my mouth and sucked on the tip of it. I then began to lick his shaft from his balls upward in a swirling motion all around his cock, pushing the neon cock ring up as I did so. I pushed the ring back down on his cock and grabbed the bottle of body paint. I squirted some in my hand then began to massage his chest. When I finished, the whole front of his body was lit up and glowing neon blue.

Now it was my turn, I laid back and he began to lick my nipples, continuously swirling his tongue around them, sucking and tugging on them at the same time. Slowly he made his way down my stomach until he got to the hairs of my pussy. He lathered them with his tongue and then made his way to my clit. He swiped my clit once then smothered it with his mouth. Dylan began to slowly suck on it to the point where my back magically began to arch up off the bed.

It was so good that he began to take my breath every time he sucked on it. I gathered myself as Dylan started to spread my legs open even wider than before. He then headed back to my clit to finish the meal he had started. It got to the point where I was about to pass out. When he was done, I looked down at him and to my surprise, he still had on the neon cock ring and it was still glowing in the dark.

He reached over and grabbed the yellow body paint and began to lick every part of my body he had not licked before. He then began to give me a massage with the body paint. It was still dark, and his body was still lit up and glowing blue and now my body was starting to come alive and take form in the color of yellow. After he finished massaging my body, he crawled on top of me. We kissed and began to grind and rub our bodies against each other, mixing the yellow paint with the blue paint. He was rock hard, and I could feel his dick throbbing against my clit and my soaking wet pussy.

Dylan slid himself inside me, and we began a glow filled game of tug of war with his dick. He pumped down, and I pumped up. I pushed Dylan off of me then he picked me up and placed my back against the wall. My legs were dangling over his arms as he held me up. I gave him soft sweet kisses on his lips as he began to thrust his dick inside of me slowly but forcefully. He opened his mouth as I licked his lips. He stuck out his tongue, and I began to suck on it. We kissed, and it was as if we were breathing as one.

Dylan removed me from the wall and just held me in his arms. I bounced up and down on his dick for a while until I could feel it deep in my stomach. He put me down and I turned to face the wall. He moved up closer behind me, pinning me between him and the wall with my arms up like I was going to be frisked. He repeatedly thrust *Luke Skywalker* deep inside me until my arms slowly slid down the wall leaving behind a yellow and blue body paint trail. My arms became limp and just dangled by my side.

It was such a turn on as I watched our glow filled bodies and especially the blue light of the cock ring disappearing deep inside my pussy then reappear in the mirror on the wall. The body paint on our bodies began to mix and blended into a beautiful bright green color. We had several more cosmic love sessions that night before we both fell on the bed exhausted.

The next morning, I woke up and Dylan was still sleeping face down on his stomach. There was dried body paint all over the sheets and smeared on the wall. I went to use the bathroom and as I headed back to the bed. It was the first time I had seen Dylan's bedroom in total daylight. On one of the walls was an amazing painted mural of some landscape that immediately caught my eye because it looked so familiar.

I walked closer, and it was just something about it. It had a tree house that seemed to draw me in even more. Dylan must have heard me walking around and woke up.

He asked, "What are you doing?

I said, "Examining this amazing mural on your wall."

He told me, "Thank you, it took me several months to complete it."

I was amazed that he could paint that good. I asked him, "Is this an actual place?"

He said, "Yes, it is, and actually it is about 20 minutes from here. One day I was riding my motorcycle and passed this land that sat abandoned, so I stopped and started taking pictures of it. When I got home, I fell in love with one of the photos, so I decided to paint a mural of it on the wall."

CHAPTER 12

Land of Dreams

I got back in the bed and laid down, but I could not stop thinking about the mural on the wall. It just reminded me of somewhere I had been before, but I just could not think of where. The mural consisted of a large field, a dilapidated old house, a swing set, a jungle gym, a treehouse, and an old weathered red barn. There was also a mailbox with no name or number on it. I asked Dylan, "Can you take me to this place?"

He said, "Of course, I can take you," then hopped up to go take a shower.

I jumped up and was right behind him. We showered together, got dressed, and headed out on his motorcycle.

On the way there everything just seemed different. The wind was blowing with all of the trees seemingly swaying in harmony. I held on tight and took in all of the beautiful scenery. It did not take us long to get there. I knew we were close when Dylan began to slow down and turned into a driveway. This is when I recognized the mailbox with no number on it. I saw the dilapidated house and we pulled up in front of it.

Dylan said, "Here we are!"

I got off the bike and saw the treehouse in the distance. Walking around felt somewhat spiritual. It was like I belonged there and this was where I was supposed to be. The sweet smell of honeysuckles filled the air as I could hear the chirping and humming of the birds, the buzzing of the bees, and an occasional croaking of a toad in the nearby creek.

The closer I got to the treehouse, the more I began to have flashbacks to my childhood. I felt like a young girl again and began to run toward it. Finally, it hit me, and I realized that this was the land Ma Lillie, and Grandpa Eddie lived on when I was a small child. There was only one way to confirm if this was true. I began to climb the ladder of the treehouse as quickly as I could. I remembered Grandpa Eddie had built the treehouse especially for me. I also remembered on several occasions having tea parties with him in there.

When I reached the top, I went inside and had to tear down some cobwebs and finally confirmed what I thought to be true. Painted on the rear wall of the treehouse were the words

"To my beloved Meadow, let your imagination run wild and may you live Free Forever! Love Grandpa Eddie."

My heart sank, and I burst into tears as I read it, it was like he was right beside me reading it with me. Dylan came in the treehouse and saw me crying.

He asked, "Are you ok? What is wrong?"

I told him, "This use to be my Grandparents land, and I spent many summers here when I was a young girl."

Dylan said "What are the chances of this happening? You mean the whole time that I was painting the landscape on my wall it belonged to your family?"

I said, "Yes."

His response was, "There has to be some divine spiritual fate that brought us together."

We climbed down the treehouse and walked along the honeysuckle bushes. I grabbed one and pulled out the stem. I held it to Dylan's lips as he opened his mouth. I told him, "Suck on the stem."

He did and said, "It tastes good. I never knew how sweet they were."

We left the honeysuckles and headed towards the house. Walking through each room, started to bring back good memories from my past. It was so weird to see some of the same original furniture still in the house. I wondered, "What happened? Why did they leave everything behind?"

I walked into my Grandparents old bedroom and opened a drawer that contained a bag that was sticking out of it. Opening the bag, I saw lots of papers and an envelope. I began to open the envelope and pulled out what I realized was a prom invitation. I thought to myself this has got to be old because I have never seen anything like this. I continued to read and realized it was definitely a prom invitation from Dad to Mom dated May 15, 1963. I put it in my pocket because I wanted to take it back and show it to Mom.

After spending some time in the house and looking through all the rooms, we went outside to the backyard. There was a swing connected to two trees. We sat down and began to talk. I began to reminisce about the summers I spent here. I could not believe that I was back at this place of so many good memories. My phone suddenly began to ring. I looked at it, and it was Mr. Stevens.

I answered and he asked, "Are you busy?"

I told him, "I am with Dylan, and we are about to head back to town."

Mr. Stevens said, "Great," and asked, "Is it possible for both of you to stop by the store on your way back? I have some business I want to discuss with both of you."

I asked Dylan, "Is it ok?"

He said, "Yes."

I told Mr. Stevens, "We will be there in about thirty minutes."

Before we got back on the bike, I turned around to take one long last look at the land and told Dylan, "It is a shame this land is just sitting here wasting away with all of my family history and love, just wasting away with it." Then we got on the bike and headed back to town.

The whole time back I continued to reminisce back to all of the fun times I had on that land and my eyes started to fill with tears. They were not tears of sadness or pain but were simply tears of joy.

We pulled into the parking lot of Mr. Stevens's store, and we could see the silhouette of him anxiously waiting inside the screen door.

He told both of us, "Come on in."

We walked in and headed to the back. We sat down at one of the nearest tables. A few minutes later we were joined by Mr. Stevens.

He said, "Thank you both for coming, I really appreciate it. First of all, Dylan, I liked your proposal for renovating the store, and I would like for you to go ahead and start work on it next week."

Dylan said, "The store will need to be closed down for about 3-4 weeks until renovations are complete."

I smiled and kissed Dylan on his cheek.

Mr. Stevens said, "There is just one thing. I would like for you to add to your new design and that would be a small bakery section in the corner of the store. It should consist of a countertop with a display case. This section will also include a microwave, an oven, a cooler, and a small storage closet." Mr. Stevens went on to tell me, "I enjoyed each and every pie and cobbler that you made for me. They all tasted just as if Ma Lillie had made them herself and I have a proposal for you."

Mr. Stevens told me, "I would like to sell the pies in my store after the renovations are complete. We will split the profits 80/20. Eighty percent for you and 20% for me but my percentage will be put into a trust account in your kid's names. The money will be for their college fund once they graduate high school."

I ran and gave him a big hug and kiss and told him, "I love you." In that moment I thought about the sign I made and just decided to give it to him at the grand reopening of the store. Dylan and I left the store, and both of us agreed today was a very good day.

The next few weeks Dylan spent most of his time renovating Mr. Stevens store. I concentrated on *Poetry and Pie* and my learning center. Business was doing great, and we got plenty of good reviews from customers. Mrs. Callaway even popped up one night making another surprise appearance and loved the show.

Finally, it was the day of the grand opening for Mr. Stevens's store. Dylan had finished remodeling a few days before, and everything had been cleaned up and put back in the store. Now, it was time for the big reveal. I bought a big yellow ribbon and tied it across the two columns on the front porch of the store. We invited several of Mr. Stevens family and friends, but it seemed like the whole town showed up. Mr. Stevens stood on the porch and thanked everyone for coming then took the scissors and cut the ribbon as everyone cheered.

I stopped him just before he was to open the door and handed him a present that was wrapped up. I told him, "It is just a little gift of appreciation from the kids and myself." He was surprised and eagerly began to tear off the wrapping paper. It was the new sign that I had created for him to go on the outside of the store.

He was elated and told me, "I love it!" He then held it up so the crowd could see it.

Mr. Stevens then turned and opened the door. Everyone rushed in and the store was immaculate. It still had the country store look and feel but with a modern-day twist on it. Mr. Stevens grabbed my hand and led me to the bakery section.

He told me, "This is where the magic will take place."

It was beautiful with a sign hanging over the counter that read *Ma Lillie's Pies*. I was so proud that Ma Lillie's legacy would live on through me.

About a week before the grand opening Mr. Stevens asked me, "Can you make 30 mini pies and cobblers of each type?"

I told him, "Yes, I can." We finished them the night before the grand opening and delivered them to Mr. Stevens that same night. The plan was to give them away free to all of the guests as samples of what is to come.

`I grabbed the kids and Mr. Stevens directed me to where the cooler was that contained all of the pies and cobblers. We took them out and began to sit them on the counter. All of the customers began to line up, and we started to give them away. Thirty minutes later all of the mini pies and cobblers were gone and everyone began to leave.

Earlier I had seen Dylan call Mr. Stevens outside. They both had put up the new sign for the store then they were outside for a long time conversing amongst themselves and greeting the guests as they left. I walked out the door and said, "What are you fine gentlemen talking about?"

They both smiled and said, "Just men talk," as they smiled at each other.

I just smiled back and shook my head as I wrapped my arms around Dylan and told Mr. Stevens, "I think the grand opening was a success."

He agreed and said, "The pies and cobblers were a hit. I think that we will only sell the mini versions of the pies and cobblers in the store and the larger pies and cobblers would be by special order only. Customers will order the bigger pies, and after their order is complete, we will special deliver them in person to the clients within a 30-mile radius from the store." He also said, "I am going to hire one of my Granddaughters to help make the pies in the store and they will be the primary person responsible for delivering the pies."

I said, "Great idea because I was wondering how I was going to juggle the lounge, the learning center, and Ma Lillie's Pies. She can come to the house for a few days, and I will swear her to secrecy and teach her how to make the pies. She will then be ready to make them on her own at the store."

Mr. Stevens said, "Well, it sounds like a plan."

I gathered the kids after hugging Mr. Stevens and giving Dylan a kiss, and we headed home for the night.

The next day my parents came over, and I could not wait to show them the prom invitation. I had bought a frame for it and placed it inside. I handed the frame to Mom and her mouth opened wide and suddenly a tear started to fall.

Mom asked, "Where did you find this?"

She called Dad over and showed it to him as she said, "Honey do you remember this?"

Dad looked and said, "Wow, you know how long ago that was?"

They looked into each other's eyes and began to kiss like it was their first kiss all over again. My heart was warm, and all I could think about was that was the type of love I wanted to have and maintain with Dylan. I felt with the love and affection we already have for each other that we definitely could get to that point.

They both asked, "Where did you find the invitation?"

I told them, "I found it in a dresser in Ma Lillie's old house."

Mom asked me, "Are you talking about the house on the land that my parents use to own?"

I said, "Yes, and no one lives there. It is just sitting there abandoned and everything is still there."

I asked Mom, "What happened? Why was it just left abandoned?"

Mom told me, "After your Grandpa Eddie died Ma Lillie decided to sell the land."

She said, "Living in the house is just too much for me to bear. Being constantly reminded of the man I loved so much, no longer being there with all of our memories replaying constantly in my mind is just a torture I do not want to experience anymore."

She decided just to sell the house and start over. She did not want to bring anything from the old house into the new house so she just left it all behind. A Middle Eastern investment company now owns the land and wanted to build a Hindu Temple on it, but it kept getting blocked by the town council.

Mom kept staring at the prom invitation and shaking her head.

Then she said, "This was the beginning of many happy years with a wonderful, loving, and kind man who I love dearly. Thank you so much!"

When they left later that afternoon, they walked to the car holding hands. Dad opened the car door, and Mom got in. She smiled and blew me a kiss. It was like finding that prom invitation intensified a fire of passion and love in them that was already burning brightly for each other.

About an hour after my parents left, the doorbell rang. It was Melissa, Mr. Stevens Granddaughter. She had arrived to begin her training of how to make Ma Lillie's pies and cobblers. She looked very young but was just a sweetheart and was eager to learn. We went through all of the recipes together, and they all came out perfect. Melissa caught on fast and seemed to be a natural. I sent her home immediately afterward so she would not be out too late on a school night. I told her, "Come back tomorrow around the same time and I will let you prepare and bake all the pies and cobblers by yourself. I will observe and give you guidance."

When Melissa came back the next day, I had everything set up and waiting for her. I observed as she carefully measured and mixed the ingredients for each pie and cobbler then placed them in the oven. While we waited for them to finish baking, Melissa and I went into the living room. We sat down and started to have a conversation about her and the future.

Melissa told me, "I love baking cakes and pies. I would bake them all the time with my Mother before she died two years ago in a car accident. My aspiration is to become a baker and one day have my own bakery."

It all began to make sense why Mr. Stevens chose her. You could just see the joy and passion on her face and in her voice as she spoke about her dreams and what she wanted.

It was about time to check on the pies and cobblers when the doorbell rang again. I told Melissa, "Go check the pies and cobblers, and I will get the door." I already knew who was at the door, because earlier I invited Mr. Stevens and Dylan over to have pie and cobbler and to give their opinions. The kids were upstairs and came running down the stairs to say hello. Mr. Stevens had gifts for them in a bag. They opened the gifts and they were two jars of honey.

He stated, "This is honey from the same beehive that you guys harvested."

Melissa came back in the room and said, "The pies and cobblers are cooling on the countertop."

I said, "Thank you baby," and told her, "Come have a seat. This is my boyfriend Dylan and of course, you know who your Grandpa is."

I explained to Melissa, "I invited them to come so they could taste your pies and cobblers and give us feedback."

Melissa smiled with a surprised look on her face but said, "Ok."

When the pies and cobblers were cooled, Melissa cut a slice of each pie and cobbler and placed a slice of each one on six different plates. Each person grabbed a plate of their own and a fork. I told everyone, "We are going to taste each slice of pie and cobbler together and then give our feedback one at a time."

It took a while, but we managed to get through the tasting and the critiques. This exercise was very informative and provided a lot of valuable feedback and tips that would improve our product. Overall, Mr. Stevens was satisfied with Melissa's progress.

He told me, "She seems to be almost ready."

I said, "Yes, and I am very happy with her progress in such a short time. After a few more sessions she will be ready." By the end of the week she was definitely ready and we began to sell the pies and cobblers in Mr. Stevens's store.

Weeks went by, and the pies and cobblers were a hit. People of the town loved them. Word of our pies and cobblers began to spread because people were coming as far away as *North Carolina* and *Texas*. We started to get so many orders that we had to hire two more people to help Melissa.

It was about noon on a Saturday when I got a call from Dylan.

He tells me, "Let's celebrate and do something special for all of the success we both have had over the past few months."

I said, "Ok," and asked, "How should I dress?"

He responded by saying, "You can wear anything you want."

I said, "Ok, I will be ready by the time you get to my place." As usual, the kids were away with my parents for the weekend. I decided to wear a beautiful royal blue blouse that was see through and showed off my cleavage. I also had on some tight jeans that hugged every inch of my butt very nicely and flared out into bell bottoms.

When Dylan arrived, he had on a Polo shirt and some jeans. I was glad because I did not want to feel like I was underdressed. I got in the truck, and we were off. My mind wondered about all the places we could be going, but it soon stopped when it looked like we were heading in the direction of Mr. Steven's farm. It turned out that I was correct in my assumption because we started to pull into the driveway of the farm.

I was not mad, but I did wonder why we were stopping here, as we made our way up the driveway there were several cars parked on both sides. The closer we got to the farmhouse I could see people sitting in chairs under a large tree that provided lots of shade for everyone.

Dylan parked the truck and told me, "Come with me," as he reached out and grabbed my hand.

I looked closer and saw my parents, some of Dylan's family from *Pennsylvania*, and family members of Mr. Stevens were all here. Dylan guided me towards them as everyone stood up and began to clap. To my surprise, there was one single chair in the direction Dylan was leading me to. It was all white and Morgan was standing beside it wearing a beautiful sundress and holding a bouquet of roses, four white, four orange, and four red.

Morgan hands the bouquet to me and Dylan tells me, "Have a seat."

The chair was facing all of the guests, and they were all clapping and cheering. All I could do was smile. I tried to take it all in but kept wondering what was really going on. Dylan stood to the side of me and took my hand. I turned and looked into his eyes as he began to speak.

He told me, "I wrote a poem for you, and I titled it, "*I Love and In Love,*" he then began to recite it to me out loud.

I Love and In Love

I Love, your flawless beauty and infectious smile...
I am, In Love, with your glowing spirit and kind heart...
I Love, the softness of your skin, wetness of your lips,
and the smell of your gorgeous hair...
I am, In Love, with your never-ending passion for life...

You are my world and my universe...
I can no longer fight or resist your gravitation pull...
It brought us together and keeps us together...
You are my sun, my moon, and all of the stars...
A day without you is a day of not living...

Meadow Roberts will you be my wife?

Suddenly Conner stands up and walks up to Dylan with a bowtie on. He places a small box in Dylan's hand and goes back to his seat beside my Dad.

Dylan got down on one knee and said, "Meadow Sky Roberts will you marry me?"

He held out his hand which contained a big diamond ring sitting in a case. Everything and everyone was so quiet. I looked deep into Dylan's eyes and without hesitation said, "Yes," and told him, "There is no other man on earth that I desire more than you!" He placed the ring on my finger. I jumped into his arms and gave him a passionate kiss.

When he put me down, everyone surrounded us and was telling us, "Congratulations!"

All of a sudden in the distance there was a large object in the air coming our way. It began to descend as it got closer to us. I then realized it was a hot air balloon.

Dylan grabbed my hand and said, "Come with me."

We ran to the hot air balloon and got inside the basket.

Dylan told the hot air balloon operator, "Carry us to the spot."

I looked at Dylan with inquisitive eyes but did not say anything. The ride and the view were spectacular as I held onto Dylan's arm.

About 30 minutes into the ride Dylan took out some binoculars and handed them to me.

He told me "Look to your right."

I took them and put the binoculars to my eyes. I was amazed at what I saw. I turned to Dylan and said, "No way, for real?"

He replied, "Yes."

What I saw was the land that my Grandparents use to own. There was a big red bow and ribbon tied to the top of the treehouse and a banner between two trees that read, "*Welcome Home!*"

Dylan told me, "I purchased the land your Grandparents use to own, and now we own it. We are going to build a new house of our dreams from scratch right here on this land that was just sitting here wasting away. We will now preserve and nurture all of the family history and especially the love this land still has to offer."

Wiping away all the tears that were falling down my face, I managed to tell him, "Thank You, for realizing how important this land is to me and my family. You have no idea how much this means to me."

Dylan responded by helping wipe my tears and saying, "I know," then held me tight.

We sailed off into the sunset, and it felt as if I had finally won at life. It had taken me several years of enduring heartache, pain, disappointment, and uncertainty, but I persevered through it all. I have found my independence, have a successful business, a real man who truly loves me for me, but the most important thing, I have found true love in my heart and peace in my soul. For the first time in my life I felt totally free!

About the Author

K. Dion was born in Durham, NC and proudly grew up in the small town of Morrisville, NC. It is also known as "Moville." It was his Grandparents land but his family lived on it too. His Grandparents had a hog farm and it became a big part of his everyday life. Him and his cousins spent countless hours working and playing in and around the hog farm. K. Dion did not get a car when he was 16 so he rode his bike almost everywhere he wanted to go, whether on the road or through trails in the woods. One of his favorite things to do growing up was to ride his bike to the local convenient store for family who would pay him. Scavenging the local dump for bicycle parts, playing basketball, and spending countless hours in the woods exploring were also on his list of favorite things to do.

K. Dion attended elementary through high school in Cary, NC then went on to attend a local Community College for Architectural Technology. He went on to eventually get a job working for one of the top homebuilders in the country. This is where he really grew as a person, learned a lot about how to deal with people, life, and how to run a business. He had a 14-year career in the field of Architecture before being laid off in 2010 due to the housing market crash. K. Dion loved Architecture, but it was not his first love.

In 2010 he decided to go in a new direction and to focus on his first love which was Graphic Design. K. Dion ended up enrolling in DeVry University and received a degree in Web Graphic Design a few years later. His dream was to start his own business. In 2012 he founded Hollow Visions. Hollow Visions is his Media company that does Graphic Design work and publishes books.

Hollow Visions was built on the foundation of hard work, determination, perseverance, belief in himself, not being afraid to fail, passion, and a will to succeed. All of the things he learned and was taught as a kid. These values and beliefs are applied to his everyday life and into Hollow Visions.

Growing up, he never had any aspirations of being a writer. He always made good grades in English and his teachers and college professors all told him that he was a good writer, especially his high school English teacher Carrie Brock who he will never forget.

Later in life, K. Dion and his girlfriend at the time were writing out an achievement list of things they wanted to accomplish before they died. One of the things on his list was to write a book. His girlfriend suggested that he write some type of erotic book. It took him several years to complete but he did it. Today he actually enjoys writing and uses it as a form of expression that allows his imagination to run wild and to be free.

I would like to thank God for giving me the special gifts of creativity and imagination. Plus, the vision and patience needed to make this project and all things possible.

Thank You Lord!

K. Dion